KAYLA WREN

Lords of Summer

BLACK CHERRY

PUBLISHING

First edition

ISBN: 978-1-8381116-0-1

Cover art by JS Designs

This book was professionally typeset on Reedsy.
Find out more at reedsy.com

For my mother, who insists on reading this book despite being told what 'reverse harem' means.

Mum—hope you like it.

Also, I'm leaving the country.

Contents

Chapter 1

"I can't believe I let you talk me into this."

Pierce stares out the passenger window, the wind lashing her dark brown hair across her cheeks. Strands catch in her shiny, plum-colored lip gloss and she swipes them away.

"Talk you into what?" I squeeze the steering wheel, practically bouncing in my seat. "A long, scorching summer at the beach? Next semester's rent sorted weeks in advance? Top dollar for a few measly hours' cleaning each day?"

Pierce snorts and turns her mahogany eyes on me. "If you think the deal is that sweet, you're out of your mind. Nothing good in this world comes free, Lay."

I burst out laughing. I can't help it. Here we are, soaring down the highway, car windows rolled down. Sunshine brightens the sparse landscape, sparkling off the cars and trucks ahead. Even the tarmac looks smooth and flawless, photo-shopped. The sky yawns wide overhead, vivid blue, dotted with fluffy white clouds.

The radio's humming. Traffic's light. For the first time in months, we're headed somewhere no one knows us. At Pembroke Bay, we'll just be two more girls among the crowds of summer revelers.

1

No rumors. No stupid, poisonous gossip making people whisper and shoot me the side-eye. For the summer, at least, I have a blank slate.

I need this. I need it so much.

"Even if the work sucks, we'll still have time to explore. You know, go to bonfires. Drink cocktails. Learn to surf."

I'm giddy at the picture I've painted myself. I don't know why, but I need Pierce to be as excited about these jobs as I am. Maybe it's because I'm the one who bugged her into applying. Or maybe it's selfishness, and I don't want her skepticism popping my happy bubble.

Either way, I blow out a hard breath and ignore the grumpy girl in the passenger seat. No, I refuse to tarnish this. I chew on my lower lip and focus on the road.

Freedom, Layla. Eight whole weeks of freedom. Don't get in your head and definitely don't make yourself roadkill before you even get there.

Pierce hums to herself and scoops up her milkshake from the cup holder. Condensation beads the paper cup and makes my mouth water. She slurps at the straw, thick chunks of strawberry clogging the tube. My own empty cup taunts me from its holder, the chocolate still sweet on my tongue.

I've never been good at pacing myself. The second I find a pleasure, I *wallow* in it.

"You can't spend the next two years running," she says quietly after a gulp. I pretend I don't hear her over the growl of the engine, but my palms become slick on the steering wheel.

See? Happiness bubble: popped.

The thing is, I'm not running. This really is the perfect summer job, and the pay should set us up for the fall. And once those eight weeks are over, I'll go back to Llewelyn College, refreshed and ready for another hellish semester.

Yeah. The college dream turned out to be more of a nightmare for me. I'd grown up picturing parties and mixers; study groups and open mic nights.

Instead, I got rumors and vicious pranks. More nights spent alone in my room than I can count.

But Layla Mackenzie does not back down from a fight. And, more to the point, Layla Mackenzie cannot afford to transfer. Plus, it would break my parents' hearts to learn that their brave, intrepid daughter struck out on her own and got torn to pieces.

I'll grit my teeth through two more years of college, through whatever horrors the Birchwood boys dream up for me.

The thought sours my stomach. At this point, how much more can they possibly do? What horrors can they concoct; how much lower can they trample me into the dirt? But even as my brain struggles to come up with new humiliations, I know down to my bones they'll deliver.

Whatever. That is eight whole weeks away, and I have deemed it Future Layla's problem.

They can't haunt my summers as well as my school year. If I let the specter of them follow me here, then they've won.

"Five more miles," I mutter, reaching over to fiddle with the radio. I flick through the channels until I land on the peppiest, most sickeningly upbeat song I can find, then I crank the volume high. Pierce rolls her eyes when I yell along with the words, tone deaf and unashamed, but slowly she cracks a grin. By the chorus, she's wailing along too, tapping her feet on the dashboard.

God, I love this girl. I love the sunshine. I even love the miles of tarmac, stretching out in front of us.

Last year battered me to within an inch of my life. There

were days when I woke up and didn't want to exist anymore. The Birchwood boys stole my hopes, my dreams, my innocence. They broke my faith in other people, and all the hard-won optimism my parents worked to instill in me.

But they're hundreds of miles away, back at Llewelyn College.

They can't hurt me here, and that means for the first time in over a year, I'm finally free.

This summer job will be perfect. It has to be.

"Holy shit."

We sit in my battered old Toyota, gaping at the house in front of us. I let the engine idle for a long moment before remembering myself and turning the key.

"Do you think they're all like this?" Pierce hisses.

I shrug, mouth suddenly dry. It's not like we haven't seen mansions before. Back at college, the big Greek houses are beasts to behold. And then, when you leave campus, there are the real mansions: the old money gems.

My tormentors live in Birchwood House: a sprawling townhouse on the rich side of town, all polished oak floorboards and soaring ceilings. Even their damn pool table is built from solid, hand-carved wood. I remember smoothing my palm over it at a party back in first year. Back before I was public enemy number one; before they'd toss me to the sidewalk if I dared show my face at a social event.

The house looming over my poor car definitely has that same old money vibe. It's built from pale brick, with balconies stretching around the second and third floors. It's a vision of power and opulence, hunkering among the manicured gardens like some kind of predator.

Pierce huffs out a breath and checks the address on her

4

phone one last time. Swiveling in her seat, she fixes me with a glare.

"Tell me what yours is like. If it's smaller, we're swapping."

I smirk, even though my cheeks feel stiff. Even after two years on campus, wandering down streets which practically ooze New England wealth, I'm still the dazed little girl from Santa Fe.

"Less cleaning?"

"Smaller egos."

I snort. "Unlikely. But deal."

I undo my seat belt and hop out to help Pierce with her suitcase. Gertie, my faithful ride, can be tempestuous on a good day. You have to bang on her trunk just right to get it open.

"I guess the clue was right there with the 'live-in maid' thing." Pierce stands with her arms crossed while I lug her case out of the trunk. I yank at the handle, huffing and cursing while she takes in her home for the next eight weeks. "Something tells me this won't be a few measly hours of cleaning, Lay."

I heave her suitcase onto the driveway, straightening up and smacking my palms together. Pierce's case is sleek and classy: burgundy with a bronze pull-out handle. My gaze slides to my own battered luggage: a zebra-print hold-all I picked up for a few bucks at the thrift store.

Damn. Why do I always have to go for the loudest, most ugly possible option?

So that one day someone will notice you, a voice whispers in my head. I crack my neck and ignore it.

"All set?" I say with forced cheeriness. I'm still determined not to give up on my summer high, but this stately house has put a dent in my confidence. What if this summer is just more of the same? Just eight more weeks of angry, rich jerks who take sick pleasure in crushing my spirit?

No. These are new people. Probably some wealthy family on vacation, who just want downtime from whatever rich people stress about. I'll work quietly in the background, and in my time off, I am getting on a damn surfboard.

Re-energized, I yank Pierce into a tight hug before gripping her by the shoulders. "I'll barely be a mile away. I checked Google Maps; you can practically walk door-to-door along the sand."

Pierce nods and spins to face the house again. Her spine straightens and her shoulders settle back. My best friend is a force to reckon with.

"Send me pictures," she throws out over her shoulder as I slam Gertie's trunk closed. "And, you know. Try to act sane."

I wink as I pull the driver's door open. "I can't think what you mean."

* * *

The five minutes alone in the car is enough to set my nerves jangling again. I lower the window and let the salty breeze sting my cheeks, squinting into the late afternoon sun to catch glimpses of the sea. We saw snatches of the coastline on the drive over, but not like this. Not so close that I can taste it on the wind.

I'm so caught up craning my neck at the ocean that I almost miss the turn for my house. My phone tells me to *turn right* in that calm, robotic voice, and I panic, slam on the brakes, and wrench at the wheel. Gertie heaves around the corner, two wheels almost leaving the ground.

Fuck. Not my finest moment. I peer at the rear-view mirror, but the road is empty. There's no blare of accusatory horns.

I creep the rest of the way down the drive, sheepish and flushed.

The house should be empty, at least, so no guests will have seen my antics. The agency was strict in its instructions: all the summer staff are to check in by 6pm today at the latest. We each go to our assigned mansions, settle into the staff quarters, and prepare for the guests' arrivals. Tomorrow, we'll meet whoever we'll be waiting on hand and foot for the next eight weeks.

I'm kind of excited. Not to clean or serve, but to meet new people. Try out a fresh, better me. You'd think the last two years at Llewelyn would have warned me off coming within half a mile of the elites, but I have a good feeling about this summer. When I pull up in front of the house—my home for the next couple of months—warmth spreads through my chest.

Yes. *Yes.* I spring out of the car and thrust my fist into the air.

"Fuck yeah!"

There's no one around, what with the private gardens stretching in both directions. I can see the neighbors' houses in the distance, but they're too far to pay any notice of me. No need to dial it in; I can skip and whoop as loud as I damn well want.

This house: this gorgeous, red brick dream, is mine.

Those huge, sparkling French doors leading onto wrought-iron balconies; those pink roses climbing the walls. These airy, fragrant gardens with their fountains and flower beds and Scandinavian-style pool house.

Yes, okay, tomorrow the proper guests will arrive and then I'll be the dutiful maid in the background. But tonight, I'm here alone. Tonight, I'm king of the castle, and this king has plans. They start with me bouncing on every single bed in this mansion and end with me floating on a lilo.

I lug my zebra hold-all out of Gertie and drag it up the driveway, juggling the handle with one hand and calling Pierce with the other.

"Tell me yours has a pool," I say without preamble. My hold-all bangs into my heel with every step and I curse, kicking back at it.

"A pool and then some." The smirk is clear in Pierce's voice, and relief loosens my chest. She likes it. Okay. I gulp down a big breath of sweet, summer air and start to clatter my way up the front steps. "You might be onto something here, Lay."

My goofy smile stretches my cheeks until they ache. "Wait, say that again. I need to record you for my ringtone."

"Nice try, dork."

I fumble for my key while Pierce waxes poetic about her house in my ear. Her deck backs directly onto the beach; she has an honest-to-God sea view, and even her little staff quarters have an en suite. I jam the key into the lock, impatient to see if I struck gold too.

"How are you marking your territory?"

"The usual," she says as I disable the alarm with the code I scrawled on an old envelope. "Peeing on the furniture. Carving my name into the headboards. You?"

It's cool inside the lobby. My sneakers squeak against the polished floor as I step forwards, gaping up at the sculpture hanging overhead. A shoal of hundreds of ceramic fish are fixed to wires, circling around the dangling bulbs. When I flick the wall switch, bright light shines through the shoal and casts gorgeous, rippling shadows on the walls.

"Lay?"

Right. Talk now; freak out later.

"Poke around, obviously. You know these mansions always have hidden rooms and shit. Then I think I'll break these beds in before my pampered guests arrive. No reason they should have all the fun."

A cold voice echoes through the lobby. "I can think of a few reasons."

No. I'd know that voice anywhere. It's not fucking possible.

I turn slowly, limbs suddenly stiff, like we really are underwater. My hand cramps from clutching my phone to my ear, but Pierce's voice is just a garbled buzz.

Eli Henderson, leader of the Birchwood boys, stands in a doorway across the lobby. His posture is relaxed, his hands in the pockets of his suit pants, but even across the room I can see the muscle ticking in his jaw.

"You," I breathe, hands falling to my sides. Behind me, my battered luggage drops to the floor with a thump. Pierce's tinny voice chatters away somewhere near my hip.

Eli's eyes narrow. He strides towards me, stopping five feet away.

"Are you stalking me?"

He bites the question out, like even talking to me is an effort. Never mind that even if I were a nut job, Eli Henderson is the last person on Earth I would stalk.

I choke out a laugh, though it comes out more like a sob. I hate that. I hate that he makes me feel like this, like I'm slow and stupid and about to burst out of my skin.

"Are you serious?" A flush starts at my neck and prickles up over my face. "Fuck that. I'm the *maid*. I came here to get *away* from you."

Eli Henderson does not like that. He rocks back and forth on his heels, sucking at his teeth like he can dig me out like a popcorn kernel.

"No," he says abruptly. He digs his phone out of his pocket and starts tapping at the screen. "This is unacceptable. You can't be here. We'll get a different maid."

For a crazy moment, I agree with him. I can't be here. My heart can't take it; it's already hammering hard enough to crack ribs. But then reality slides back in, and I remember I need this job.

Money. Rent. The fucking necessities of life. We sublet our apartment back on campus, and this job was supposed to cover next semester's rent.

"Wait," I croak, but he's already lifting his phone to his ear. He holds up a palm and turns away, barking instructions at some agency employee. Words like 'security concern' and 'conflict of interest' drift down the hall as he strides away.

I roll my eyes, throat tight. *Conflict of interest.* I'm a maid, not a fucking lawyer. I should chase after him, swallow my pride and plead for my job, but my feet are rooted in place.

The lobby is quiet except for my ragged breathing, and I glance down at my phone screen. Dark. Pierce must have hung up. She's probably strolling around her gardens, or swimming in the pool.

For a sick, selfish moment, I think about dragging my bag back to Gertie. I could tear out of here, pull up at Pierce's house and ask her to come back with me. Get her to leave her gorgeous mansion and this stretch of golden sand and come live in my car until we find a rental back at campus.

She'd do it, too, if I asked. That's why I can't. I won't ruin her summer like that. Not when I dragged her here.

Fucking hell.

I put my shoulders back and tip my chin up. Eyes closed, I draw in a breath through my nose, then hold it for a moment.

I can do this. I can figure something out. There will be a restaurant or a bar I can work in; I can sleep in Gertie or camp on the beach.

My breath gusts out, long and hard.

Eli Henderson. The ringleader of the Birchwood boys. The guy who made my second year at college miserable. The guy who kept me up sobbing into my pillow so many nights; who spread the worst rumors about me and made the whole campus hate me on sight.

Eli led the Birchwood boys in an unholy crusade against me. He lost me my gallery internship and got me mobbed out of student dorms.

And now he's here.

I realize with a jolt we're alone in this house. There's no one nearby to hear if I scream.

Eli's never threatened me physically. Never tried to push me around. But there's no chance in hell I'm gambling my safety on trusting this piece of shit.

I storm back out to Gertie, to barricade myself away and think of Plan B.

Chapter 2

Something shoves against my shoulder and I stumble back. All around, bodies press close and jostle, laughing and tipping back drinks. Music drips heavy through the sound system, and the bodies grind against each other, hands roaming. It's so loud each thump of bass rattles my teeth.

I squint down at my phone, swaying. Nothing from Pierce. She must be here somewhere—she was just here, we were drinking together—

A shoulder slams into my back, jarring my phone out of my grip. It clatters to the floor, lost to the tangle of limbs and the empty bottles littering the parquet tiles.

"Hey!"

I swing around, stumbling as I go, all set to give this clumsy asshole a mouthful.

My words shrivel up and die in my throat.

Eli Henderson glares down at me, spite churning in his eyes. Two spots of color burn high on his perfect cheekbones: a testament to the hatred for me heating his blood. A Birchwood boy flanks him on each side, their arms folded and jaws clenched like well-moneyed bouncers.

"Who let the trash in?"

Eli's voice is smooth and steady, at odds with the shake in his

12

fingers. They ball into fists when I glance down, and he shoves his hands in his pockets like he can't trust himself not to wring my neck.

Hurt crackles through my chest and stings my eyes. I can't help it. I've never been hated like this.

I don't know how to make it stop.

I suck in a shaky breath, my eyes flicking between the three of them. Eli Henderson, Maddox Landry, and Jasper Wood. I send up a quick 'thank you' to the universe that Nate Becker, the fourth and most savage Birchwood boy, isn't here.

"I was invited," I grit out. It's a miracle they can hear me over the thumping music and raucous laughter, but Eli's mouth thins.

"Let me take care of that." His words are courteous, like he's offering to carry my bags or pick up my tab. But I know even before he plunges into the crowd that Eli Henderson is not looking to do me any favors.

I'd cut my losses and get out, leave before he hurts me any worse, but my phone is still on the floor. I ignore the smirks of the two boys in front of me and swipe my dark red hair back on my forehead. Holding it there, I scan the tiles, kicking crumpled solo cups away as panic slithers through my veins.

The flash of silver glints under a nearby table, safe from the herd of trampling feet. I push over and drop to my knees, crawling to snatch at my phone. My fingertips snag the corner just as a leather brogue comes down hard, narrowly missing my fingers. When the shoe moves away, cracks spider web across the screen.

Jasper Wood squats beside me, scooping up my phone and brushing a broad thumb over the ruined glass. He turns it on its side and taps the corner on the tiles; a sliver of screen pops free, then another. My phone of five years—the phone my grandma bought me—crumbles apart in his hand.

"Whoops," Jasper says cheerfully. He hands me what's left of my phone, chucking me under the chin with his knuckle. When he stands up and walks away, I stay kneeling, head ducked. A tear rolls free, sliding down my cheek, as I try the power button.

Blotchy light flickers across what's left of the screen, then darkness. Nothing.

Those shits.

I don't have time to pull myself back together, because then the bone-rattling music stops. I blink up, wild-eyed and crumpled on the floor. A doe in headlights.

Drunken voices call out for more music, but a hush settles even the football crowd. Eli Henderson stands on a chair, his toned chest and shoulders above the crowd, and when Eli Henderson wants quiet, he gets it.

"Happy Friday, people," Eli begins. Cheers meet his words, and a gracious smile curls his lips. He lifts a hand; quiet settles over the room once more.

And me? I will myself to sink into the tiles. I should force my legs into action; push myself up and flee while I can. But my hand trembles around my broken phone, and my breaths come short, and all the sounds in the room are coming from far away.

"It's been a rough week, right?" Eli asks, and drinks go up. Heads nod. "But finals are over!"

Whoops fill the room, louder than the music had been, and those drinks are knocked back. Next to me, a girl staggers as she drinks, dripping a stream of beer onto my lap. The stain spreads over my yellow dress, looking for all the world like I've pissed myself.

Suddenly Eli's eyes find mine, and it's like we're the only ones in the room. My chest shudders as I heave in a breath, and I give the tiniest shake of my head.

It doesn't matter. It never does. He smirks, face bright with malice,

14

and his next words make bile rise up my throat.

"If anyone needs stress relief, we have our beloved campus whore ready and waiting on her knees. Give us a wave, Layla!"

Hungry eyes find me, stained and queasy. Next to me, one of the football guys reaches for me like he's going to use me right here in front of everyone. He has his own beer stain, matching mine, splattered right down the front of his jersey.

"We have our first taker!" Eli calls to a fresh round of cheers, then the music blares again. I bat the footballer's hand away and stagger to my feet, stomach lurching. He swipes for me again, rougher this time, and I lunge out of reach. The football crowd jeers and sweaty hands paw at my back, my legs, my hair. Someone presses a wad of gum into my hair and it bounces wet against my cheek.

Out. I have to get out. I spin, unsteady on my heels, and elbow my way to the door.

Maddox Landry and Jasper Wood block the doorway, grinning at the gum in my hair. Part of me wants to yank it out, hair and all, and press it against Jasper Wood's stupid fancy waistcoat. I could drive it right into the silk; ruin something of his like he wants to ruin me.

I don't, though. The boys frown like they know what I'm thinking, drawing their hands out of their pockets, so I push my way between them instead, driving my elbows out hard.

One of them grunts, but I don't slow down. I fight my way out of that house like I'm drowning at the bottom of a pool and clawing my way towards oxygen.

I should never have come. I knew the Birchwood boys would not allow it.

They won't stop until they break me completely.

* * *

15

Knuckles rap against the car window; I jolt out of my haze. A woman wearing nude lipstick frowns at me, slumped in the driver's seat. My hands are clenching the steering wheel so hard I've lost feeling in my fingers.

I haven't thought about that night in months—I try to send the memory of each Birchwood boys torture straight to the recycle bin in my brain.

The woman raps again, raising her penciled eyebrows. She jerks her head towards the house, then she's off, marching up the drive in her skirt suit and sensible heels.

The agency. That asshole really got me fired.

I knew he would, of course. Eli Henderson does not make empty threats—I know that better than anyone. Still, I have to force my throat to swallow. Every time, these boys come up with a shiny new cruelty, and every time it knocks me sideways.

There's no point going in. No lux rental agency will side with the maid over a guest. I tip my head back against the headrest, close my eyes, and get back to scheming.

Think, Layla. There's always a Plan B. And a Plan C, D, E, all the way to the end of the alphabet. Mom and Dad did not raise me to fold at the first sign of trouble.

A heavy palm smacks against Gertie's roof, making me jump for the second time in five minutes. Eli Henderson glares through the passenger window, jaw clenched so hard I can practically hear his molars crack.

"Are you deaf?" he snaps, voice muffled through the glass. "Get back inside."

Authority rings through every word, and I'm out of the car and halfway up the steps before I even think to argue. I hate that he barks out orders like that, and I hate even more that I respond. That I jump to attention, goosebumps rippling over my skin.

The agency woman stands at the foot of the stairs, a folder perched on the banister.

"Layla Mackenzie, correct? A recent hire?"

She flicks her eyes over me before fixing them on Eli. He enters behind me and crosses immediately to the stairs, hands relaxed and stride loose. He belongs here, with his tailored clothes and flawless, rich-person complexion.

I scuff the toe of my sneaker on the polished floor.

"Thank you for giving this matter your personal attention," Eli says. "I appreciate you have much better things to be doing on a Saturday night."

The agency lady laughs and flutters a hand over her chest. She must be at least ten years older than Eli. Gross.

"Hardly! Just a lonely evening for one, I'm afraid."

Eli's mouth quirks. "I find that hard to believe."

Ugh. I mime throwing up in my mouth, but Eli catches the movement. The smile slides clean off his face, and he presses his lips together in a firm line.

"The issue, ah…"

"Georgia, please."

"The issue, Georgia, is that Layla and I are acquainted." Eli shoots me a nasty smile before strolling closer. "I'm afraid in the past Layla here has shown herself to be… unreliable."

Georgia frowns at me, then picks up her binder and starts paging through.

"We conduct rigorous background checks, Mr. Henderson. Layla's references were spotless, as with every staff member we employ." She offers him the binder, as though Eli might like to read the glowing praise from my last boss. He tips his

17

chin down, a slight smile playing across his lips.

Like this is funny to him. Like he, the moneyed brat who has never had to work a day in his life, isn't making me homeless over a stupid grudge.

"I assure you, I am an excellent worker." I shoot Eli my own sugary smile. If I have to listen to this, I will make it clear who's the asshole in the room. I turn to him, hands clasped in front of me like a good little maid, just catching Georgia's approving nod in the corner of my eye.

"I am experienced in cleaning, catering, and silver service. I'm here to make your stay as smooth as possible; you won't even notice I'm here."

I know damn well this job is a lost cause. But I'm not going to just stand there and let him paint me as the villain.

Eli pinches the bridge of his nose. "Nevertheless," he begins—

"The agency holds its staff to impeccable standards," Georgia cuts in. Huh. Guess she wasn't as flustered as she let on. "And we have a very supportive complaints procedure. While I can certainly arrange for a replacement maid, Mr Henderson, our full-time staff are all deployed. It may take up to forty-eight hours to recruit a replacement."

Forty-eight hours—*two entire days*—of pampered Eli Henderson having to fend for himself? I suppress a snort, but I must make some noise because Eli shoots me a look of pure loathing.

"Perhaps," Georgia goes on, "given your shared history, you will find Layla even more attentive than our other staff. In fact," she raises an eyebrow at me, "I'd bet her job on it."

Ugh. Fuck that. And fuck this bitch. I roll my eyes and look back at Eli.

18

Come on, I urge him with my stony glare. *Get this shit show over with.*

But Eli smirks, interest sparking in his gaze at the defiant jut of my chin.

"Of course. You're right."

Unease slithers down my spine, and I open my mouth to tell them to shove it. I don't need this fucking job that badly. I'd rather be homeless than serve Eli Henderson drinks.

"Everyone deserves a second chance, don't they?" he continues. "And I'm sure Layla here is keen to make amends."

I frown and jerk my head, but Eli won't stop fucking talking.

"My apologies for this inconvenience, Georgia." He ushers the agency rep out of the lobby, oozing charm, assuring her again and again that yes, he won't hesitate to fire me should I disappoint. Yes, he'll keep a log of his valuables.

Lovely.

The door clicks shut, and it's just the two of us in this huge, cold house. We haven't been alone since—

No. I slam that memory back in its box.

Eli keeps one hand pressed against the front door as he turns, like he's afraid I might try to run.

He's not wrong. I'm not planning on spending another fucking minute in his presence.

When Eli smiles, it reminds me of Shark Week.

"I was hasty, Layla. My apologies."

I shift from foot to foot. "Shove it, Eli. I'm not being your fucking maid."

Eli pushes away from the door, strolling to stand an arm's length away from me. His black hair curls over his forehead, and the memory of twining a lock of that hair around my finger slams into my chest. I can remember the exact silky feel

19

of it, sliding through my fingertips.

I push the thought away. Who gives a fuck if his hair's soft? Eli Henderson is the devil.

"I'll make it worth your while," he says bluntly.

I scoff. "There's not enough money in the world, prick."

His lips press together, and his gaze drags over my worn clothes, my frizzy, windswept hair.

"Everyone has a price." His words are bitter. "Name yours, and I'll pay it."

"Why?"

Seriously, who in their right mind wants someone who hates their guts on their staff? Where the fuck is this guy's self-preservation instinct? There are *knives* in this house. Cleaning bleach.

If I work here, he'll be lucky to come out alive.

Eli shrugs, like it's perfectly reasonable to offer your arch-enemy a blank check to wait on you all summer.

"Just a little game with myself. I want to see what it takes to break you."

Right. Because I'm so fucking fragile that he can destroy me on a whim.

I don't think so. But I *do* like the sound of that blank check.

"Ten thousand dollars." There must be actual limits to this offer, and I don't want to call his bluff. That kind of money would change my life; would change my parents' lives. "On top of the usual tips."

I smirk at Eli, and he rolls his eyes. I think tipping me bothers him more than the ten thousand.

"Deal," he says, way too easy.

Fuck. Should have asked for more. But it's too late now, and I'm in this. The battle lines are drawn.

"I'll turn down a room for you…" I begin to say, but he's already shaking his head, biting back a grin. My stomach churns. If there's one unchangeable rule of nature, it's that when Eli Henderson is happy, I'm about to suffer.

He leans in close, even though we're utterly alone. His breath ghosts over my neck and stirs my hair.

"I forgot to mention," Eli murmurs. His voice is like the smoothest Belgian chocolate. My breaths come faster even as a knot tightens in my core. I hate the heat building between my thighs.

"It won't just be me, Layla. The others are coming too."

Fuck. My bargaining skills are awful.

Ten thousand was a low-ball, even just for Eli. With all four of them here, my life will be hell. No way is this worth it.

"Ten thousand each," I blurt. "Or I'm not doing it. God knows you'll make me earn every cent."

Eli hums, sliding the tip of one finger down my arm. Forty thousand dollars is probably spare change to him; his family is one of the richest on the east coast.

I'd never have dared to ask for so much, but at this rate I'll need it all. The Birchwood boys can fund the therapy I'm going to need.

Even though he's good for it, Eli still drags it out. Makes me squirm.

"Done," he says finally. "Forty thousand. At the *end* of the summer."

I stagger away, out of his grasp. The room lurches, and panic squeezes my chest.

What the fuck have I done? How can any amount of money be worth this?

But how can I possibly back out now? They'd have beaten

21

me before we'd even started. It would be so much sweeter to take their money and sail through this summer, plastering an indifferent mask over my face.

Yes. Let them think they're nothing to me. Not even worth a spare thought.

They don't need to know how much even the thought of them torments me.

Eli digs his phone out of his pocket and strolls to the staircase, glancing back over his shoulder as he goes.

"Better catch your breath while you can, Layla. You belong to us now."

* * *

I drag my hold-all around the house in a daze, looking for the staff quarters. Every squeak of a floorboard, every distant thump makes me freeze in place, ears straining. Once I'm sure Eli isn't about to slink through a doorway or manifest in the shadows like a vampire, I shuffle on, pulse thundering.

I've really done it this time. Tied myself up in a neat little bow and thrown myself to the wolves.

Finally, after what feels like miles of polished floorboards and art deco rugs, I find a narrow staircase at the back of the house. Clattering down those steps is like entering a different building, and I guess in a way it is. The staff accommodation is a sparse annex, nestled in the gardens rather than facing the beach.

No ocean view for me, then. Figures.

The decor is much simpler than the main house, but I prefer it. Rather than elaborate chandeliers and original oil paintings, the annex has Edison bulbs and plain, white-washed walls.

22

It's less to take in, after the tiny campus apartment I shared with Pierce. In here, my brain has... more space, or something. Room to process.

"Anyone home?"

I don't call too loud—I don't want to disturb the psycho upstairs, after all—but my voice bounces off the annex walls. Huh. Empty.

I drag my bag past a cramped galley kitchen and a compact living space with a squashy sofa. For a stupid moment, I'm surprised, but what did I expect? It's not like the maid can microwave herself a bag of popcorn and kick back to watch a movie with the guests.

This is so much better. I grin, the knot in my chest loosening as I poke my head into a yellow-tiled shower room and head for the last few doors. Maybe I can sneak a bit of a vacation after all. It's like my own private beach rental... that just happens to be next door to my work.

I try two door knobs but they're both locked. Unused bedrooms, maybe? This house is so huge that I kind of expected a full staff living here—cooks and gardeners and so on. But hey, if I get this sweet little annex all to myself, I am *not* going to complain.

The last door in the hallway opens, and I find my bedroom for the next eight weeks. There's a bare mattress on a twin bed frame, pushed against the wall, with pillows and bedding folded on top. An oak bedside cabinet holds a lamp, a digital alarm clock, and a tiny cactus in a blue and white ceramic pot.

Moisture brims in my eyes at that damn cactus.

"Now we're talking," I whisper to myself. I drop my bag and cross the room in three strides, bending over to inspect the plant closer. "We'll call you... Calvin."

The way he's shriveled in his soil, Calvin looks a little worse for wear. His pot is tucked away here in the corner—no way the sun can really reach him. I scoop him up and cross to the windowsill, placing Calvin right up against the glass.

"There you go, buddy. We'll both work on our tans."

The longer I'm away from Eli, the more my happiness creeps back. I hum as I make my bed and inspect the rest of my tiny room, with its closet, tiny writing desk and single shelf above the bed. Whoever last stayed in this room left a few battered paperbacks: a self-help book, an airport thriller, and what looks like an old school pirate romance.

"Jackpot."

I slide it off the shelf and trace a fingertip over the wrinkled cover. My touch follows the cheek, chest and abs of the shirtless hero. His bare feet are spread, his leather pants sliding off his hips, and the wind billows in his luxurious hair.

The swooning heroine sits in a puddled white dress, clutching at the pirate's thigh.

Easy, girl.

It's not like that in real life. Not in my limited experience. In real life, the hero toys with the heroine, gets her weak and wanting, and then punishes her for it. On and on and on, until the heroine can feel bits of her soul crumbling away every time she sees him.

Yeah. Eli Henderson really did a number on me.

I toss the paperback on my bed, anyway. A girl can dream.

If today had gone to plan, I'd have the house to myself right now. The agency never mentioned early arrivals.

I should be settling in, reading about sexy pirates, maybe going for a dip in the pool. Instead, I dig an agency uniform out of my hold-all and hold it up for inspection.

It's creased all to hell, but at least it's not some hideous French maid deal. If it were, and I had to dress like that for the Birchwood boys... I'd have to leave the country.

No, this black dress reaches to my knees, hugging my legs with its soft, stretchy material. It has capped sleeves, and a white Peter Pan collar sits at the neckline. I throw the dress on, then dig my two spare uniforms out too and hang them in the closet.

The rest will have to wait. I glance sadly around my room, my little patch of paradise away from the battlefield upstairs. I'm just sliding my black lace-ups on when the slam of car doors floats through the open window.

Okay. Shit, okay. I plant myself in front of the smudgy, wall-mounted mirror and frown at my reflection.

"The Birchwood boys are demon spawn," I tell the pale girl in the mirror. "They have trust funds in place of personalities. And because of that, you're going to cash in."

I could go on, but low voices float through the gardens.

Time to go to work. And to war.

To understand the Birchwood boys, you need to see all four of them together. They're perfectly synchronized, moving parts of a whole, flowing around each other like they're dancing to their own tune. I watch them reunite in the lobby, pressed up against the wall in the shadows.

Eli is the leader—his father is a senator, so Eli has that old money, political family vibe. Tennis courts and dinner parties; schmoozing at the White House. You know the drill.

He'll probably follow in dear old dad's footsteps: he has that instinct to survey a room and take charge. Not to mention a thirst for blood. And the other guys are happy for him to lead, apparently—even when Eli's leadership means ruining my life.

Jasper Wood, the murderer of innocent phones, is the first through the door. Brown leather luggage in hand, Jasper looks like a *gentleman.*

Looks can be deceiving.

His parents are English, Shakespearean actors-turned-directors, and it's rubbed off on everything from his clothes to his accent. He's always clad in tailored shirts and waistcoats, like he's wandered out of a regency novel, his wavy blond hair tousled like he's just back from breaking in a stallion.

Jasper used to remind me of a sexy librarian, or an Austen hero, back before he set out to make my life hell. Now I just think he's an ass.

Nate Becker is next through the door, barging it open like the hunk of wood insulted his family. With his cropped inky hair, sharp cheekbones, and the stubble coating his jaw, Nate Becker looks sharp. Feral. A wolf among the flock.

He tosses his head back with a grin when he sees Eli, and an earring winks against his olive skin.

"Come here, you dickhead," Nate says, and then he and Eli collide in one of those back-slapping, *man* hugs. Eli grips his elbow and murmurs in his ear, and Nate snorts.

"Thought you'd like your gift."

So Nate is responsible for the death of my summer. Yep: that checks. He's always been single-minded in his hatred, in his pursuit of the last of my joy.

I wonder idly if the Birchwood boys even like the coast, or if Nate dragged them here solely to fuck with me.

I don't know how the hell he knew I was coming here, but it's not like it matters. These guys have the whole campus eating out of their hands; information is easy for them to come by.

Eli shoves Nate's shoulder, a bit too rough to be playful.

Guess he doesn't enjoy being kept in the dark.

One side of Nate's mouth ticks up, baring his teeth. I press my clammy palms against the wall and pray for just a few more moments of peace.

Maddox Landry is the last inside, closing the door gently behind him. Maddox is the calm to Nate's storm, a soothing presence I used to seek out before they all turned on me. Not that Maddox and I were friends, but I knew who he was, and I liked sitting near him in the quad.

There's one bench that he seems to favor, and he lounges there on sunny days between classes. Sometimes he swigs from a coffee cup, throat working; other days he lays flat on the bench, head pillowed on his arm while he reads.

Before he hated me too, I'd go looking for Maddox on bad days. Not in a stalker kind of way—more like a lonely stray cat. Maddox is so calm that it radiates out from him and soothes passersby.

That's what I used to think, anyway. These days, he's often the reason my day has gone so wrong.

The boys grasp elbows and slap each other on the back, talking about the drive and the house and whatever else. I'm not listening. No: I'm gazing at the effortless way they move together—the relaxed, open looks on their faces—with dread.

It used to make me sick with envy, before everything. The way they clearly *belonged.* I'm sure that's half of why they're so damned confident; why everyone bows to their every whim.

They've found their brothers. I can't think of four people who deserve it less.

And I'm not just jealous: it's a self-preservation thing. Individually, they're bad enough, but when they're all together, everything is amplified. Including their hatred for me.

27

Especially that.

"Layla, darling." I slam my eyes shut. It's like Eli heard my quickening breaths. "Come and greet your guests."

Nate already knows what's coming, the asshole, his eyes bright and eager. He spins on his heel to scan the room, lighting up when he sees me. Jasper and Maddox frown at each other, clearly out of the loop.

Their faces go blank the second I step forward.

"Welcome to Pembroke Bay," I whisper, then clear my throat. "I'll be serving you this summer." I flush bright, angry red at my choice of words, but force myself to carry on with the agency's script. "Please let me know if you require any assistance and I will be happy to help."

Maddox cocks his head to the side, while Eli lounges against the staircase banister.

"I bet you fucking will," Nate snarls, and the rest of them smirk.

I force out an even breath and clasp my hands together in front of my dress. "Will you require anything this evening, *sirs*?"

I throw the full depth of my loathing for them, my revulsion, behind that word.

Jasper grunts and shakes his head, not as amused as Eli and Nate. He snatches up his suitcase and takes to the stairs, skipping two steps with each stride. Maddox follows, throwing me a warning look as he goes.

Like this was my idea, somehow. Asshole.

"What do you think, Nate?" Eli circles slowly behind me, but I keep my eyes glued on the wall opposite. "Do you require anything from Layla?"

Nate steps close, so close I can smell the fresh sea air on his shirt from the drive. His brown eyes drop to my shoes and drag slowly up my body, darting to every crease and flaw. He looks me in the eye and sneers, the tip of one tooth digging into his lip.

"I want her to call me sir again."

I swallow hard. When Eli murmurs in my ear from behind, I flinch but stay rooted to the spot.

"Come along, little maid." His palm claps down hard on my shoulder, giving me a shake. "Earn your wage."

"Enjoy your stay, *sir*," I spit at Nate.

His eyes darken.

"Oh, I will. Count on it, Mackenzie."

By the time their footsteps disappear up the stairs, I've held my breath for so long my lungs burn.

Chapter 3

"**A**re you *insane*?"

Pierce is shrill in my ear, and I hold the phone away with a wince.

"Those assholes hate your guts! They *ruined* second year for you, Layla! And you're going to bow and scrape to them for some stupid summer job?"

"For forty thousand dollars," I correct. "And to prove I don't give a shit."

"But you do give a shit!" Pierce shoots up an octave, and I sigh down the phone. Level-headed under stress, my best friend is not.

I press two fingers to my temple. "I know. I know, okay? It's a terrible fucking idea and they're going to make my life hell. I just..."

I trail off, glancing around my sweet little bedroom. Early morning sun spills through the window, and roses from the flowerbed outside tickle at the gap below the glass.

I love this little room. Last night, I found a quilt folded up in the wardrobe, with blue and yellow patchwork squares and little sequins sewn on. The flash of color on my bed made my bruised heart sing.

Then there's Calvin. The cactus has already perked up in

the sun.

At least one organism is glad I'm here.

"Pierce, I can't let them win again."

My room in student dorms; the internship in the art gallery that I hustled so hard for. So many parties I missed out on, so many classes I hid at the back of the lecture hall and made sure never to raise my hand. These boys stole so much from me already.

They've made me docile. Weak.

"Lay…" Pierce murmurs, and I can hear her pity through the phone. I grit my teeth—a knee jerk reaction, anger bubbling up in my throat—but I take a deep breath and force my jaw to unlock. None of this is Pierce's fault, and she stuck by me at college when no one else would.

"It'll be fine." I inject false cheeriness into my voice, trying to convince myself as much as my best friend. "It's probably a blessing in disguise. I bet they barely call for me, they hate the sight of me so much. I'll be kicking back on the beach, having a leisurely summer while you chase around after spoiled kids."

"They're actually pretty cute."

Pierce's guest family arrived first thing this morning: a couple in their thirties with three young children in tow. Pierce said they rolled up in a Landrover with Burberry car seats in the back.

"Say that again after bath time," I tease, but really I'd give anything to swap her sticky toddlers for the fully grown brats upstairs.

"You can change your mind at any point, Lay. I'll bail with you, no questions asked. I don't give a fuck what those guys think, and you shouldn't either."

A smile tugs my lips for the first time since the last three

Birchwood boys arrived. What did I ever do to deserve this girl?

"Sure thing. I love you, you know that?"

Her scoff is like static on the line. "Keep it in your pants, Lay."

My bedroom door slams open, bouncing off the wall. I freeze, my retort stalling on my tongue.

Eli Henderson fills my narrow doorway, expression blank as he takes in every detail of my sparse, threadbare room. Compared to the luxury upstairs, this must look like a prison cell. The smirk that curls his mouth confirms it.

"Time to work, Miss Mackenzie. I wouldn't expect you to know this, but it's customary for the help to be up and ready well before the guests rise."

Eli's dark eyes skate over my tangled red hair, my loose pink tank top and cherry-print pajama shorts. "Irony upon irony," he breathes, staring at the little red fruits dotted on the cream fabric, before looking up and arching an eyebrow.

"I'll call you later," I mutter, hanging up before Pierce can yell insults at Eli through the tiny speakers. When I toss the phone on my bed and he makes no move to leave, I raise my chin. "I need to change into my uniform."

"Oh, I don't think that will be necessary." Eli takes my elbow between finger and thumb, like he's picking up an especially gross piece of garbage. He tugs me into the hallway, pulling the door shut behind us and spinning a key in the lock before I can blink.

"Where did you get that?" I splutter, barging past him to tug at the doorknob. It rattles, loose in its socket, but the door doesn't budge. I stand in the cool corridor, slate tiles cold beneath my bare feet, gaping up at the asshole in front of me.

Eli holds up the key, turning it in his elegant fingers to peruse all its angles. He's clad in tailored navy pants and a fitted white shirt open at the collar. Even on vacation, he doesn't know how to relax. Suddenly, my loose tank top and pajama shorts feel like hardly any clothing at all.

Goosebumps prickle over my exposed skin. I cross my arms over my chest, keenly aware I'm not wearing a bra. Eli glances down, and with the way his jaw tightens, I *know* he sees the way my nipples have pebbled under my top.

"I won't work for you half-naked."

Eli tilts his head to one side. "You've offered to do worse before. I assure you, Mackenzie, nothing could make a less tempting sight."

My cheeks flush at his words, but I barrel on.

"The agency—"

"Will be most disappointed to hear of your attitude this morning. Oversleeping, locking yourself out of your room, and now trying to seduce your guests by wandering around like... that."

He gestures up and down my body, nose wrinkling in disgust.

"You're a pig, you know that?"

"A pig holding the literal key to your future."

Humiliated tears burn at the back of my eyes, but I blink hard, forcing them away. I've always been a fucking crier. Every possible emotion: happy, sad, angry, scared—I well up. I hate it.

When I open my eyes again, Eli is watching me like a snake watching a mouse.

"What do you *want*, Eli?"

"I want you gone," he says immediately, like it's obvious, like it should go without saying. Like they're not the ones who followed *me* here. "I want to win. But first, I want to break you."

He steps forward until the leather of his shoes is a hair's width from my bare toes. The highest button that's fastened on his shirt is level with my eyes, a couple of inches below his collarbone. I watch that button rise and fall with his breath, the visible sliver of his chest smooth and sculpted.

"When you leave, Layla—and you will leave—I want you feeling like less than the dirt on my shoe. I want you haunted by the money that could have changed your life, if only you weren't so fucking fragile."

"Why?" I grit out, those tears threatening again.

Eli tilts my chin up with one finger, staring at my watering eyes like he can make those tears fall out of sheer will. "Why ever not?"

I rip my chin out of his grip and stalk down the corridor. He wants to humiliate me, make me feel small, parade my body in front of his asshole friends?

Fine. Let him try. The game is on.

* * *

Any hope I had that the other Birchwood boys are still asleep is crushed when I storm into the guest kitchen. Nate sits on the counter, clad only in wine-red sweatpants which ride low on his hips and hug his muscled thighs. His bare feet kick at the cupboards, and he raises an eyebrow when I barrel through the doorway.

For a split second he pauses, a spoonful of cereal halfway to his mouth. He cradles a china bowl against his bare chest, and my gaze snags on the tattoo sprawling over his skin.

Then Nate throws his head back and roars with laughter.

"You make it so fucking *easy*, Mackenzie. Do you get all your pajamas from Playboy?"

"Fuck off, Becker."

He points his spoon at me, vicious and gleeful.

"That's 'sir' to you."

"Fuck off, *sir.*"

Across the open plan living room, Jasper groans as he stumbles through the doorway. He's wearing blue tartan sleep pants and a tight white t-shirt, and his blond hair sticks up at the back.

It'd be cute on anyone else.

Jasper Wood is not fucking cute.

He catches sight of me mid-yawn, his handsome features warped, as I gather dirty cups to load in the dishwasher. My stomach tenses at the way his face sours, an angry flush creeping over his cheeks, but I keep working.

"Good lord. What sort of maid is she, exactly?"

Nate cackles. I can't help it; I glance down and see my nipples pebbled against my thin tank top. Humiliation floods through me, hot and sickly, and I tug the dishwasher open with more force than necessary.

"A locked-out one," I spit.

Even the dishwasher in this house is huge and sparkling: top of the range. My messy, tangled hair drags through the crusted old food as I load the plates, and I curse, straightening to slam a drawer open. It only takes a minute to braid my hair over one shoulder and tie it off with some kitchen string.

Screw you, assholes. You're not ruining my hair as well as my morning.

Nate and Jasper sprawl on a corner sofa at the other end of

the room, chuckling with each other. I breathe out a sigh of relief and get back to work scrubbing countertops and cleaning up spills.

The joke's on these assholes: they can snipe and laugh all they want. I'm the one getting paid.

I don't care what they think of me. I haven't for a long time.

Maddox walks in the closest doorway, but he stands stock still when he gets an eyeful of all my bare skin. He frowns at my legs for a long moment, then leaves the way he came.

Good. That's one less dickhead to ignore.

I'm too optimistic. Five minutes later, Maddox strides back in, shoulder-length brown hair tucked behind one ear. His honey-colored eyes narrow as he throws a bundle of green fabric in my direction. It lands in a heap at my feet, and I prod it with my toe.

"Put them on," Maddox grinds out. Normally, his voice is deep and rich with a Southern tang. When he speaks to me, it's hard. "No one wants to see that."

He gestures to my body, the same way Eli did in the annex hallway. Then he brushes past me to dig through the fridge, fetching a frying pan and a pack of bacon like I'm not even here.

"I don't want to fucking show it to you, but here we both are."

I pull off the yellow rubber gloves I found under the sink and crouch to pinch the green bundle. When I stand, a stained and holey pair of canvas overalls dangle in front of me. The musky scent is cloying as hell—it makes my nose wrinkle—but if he means this to be a punishment, then the joke's on him.

I'll take Maddox's moldy overalls over Eli's forced striptease any day.

I step into those bad boys, buttoning up to my chest bone and rolling the pant legs and sleeves. When I turn, I find Maddox watching me, a slight crease in his forehead.

"Thanks," I say with a wink, and his frown deepens. "Your bacon's burning."

It's a minor victory, but I'll take it. I grab my rubber gloves and practically skip out the doorway.

* * *

After a full year of torment at college, I am damn good at making myself scarce. Even trapped in this beach-side mansion with no one but the Birchwood boys for company, I make it through the whole day without having to be in the same room as them again. I clean, launder and organize out of view, darting from room to room and peeking through cracks in the doorway to check the coast is clear.

Fuck you, Eli. You've just bought yourself one hell of an expensive maid.

I do a great job, too. If the guys want to complain to the agency, they won't get any evidence of sloppy work from me. By the time I'm done, the entire house is spotless and there is a pitcher of fresh lemonade on the kitchen counter.

I go easy on the sugar, though. Wouldn't want them mistaking it for a peace offering.

The one place I don't go is their bedrooms. Not yet. I'm taking a stand here, but I'll need to build up to that.

With my tormentors out of sight and out of mind, I remember why I was so excited for this job. The huge, sparkling windows in every room look out either to the gardens or the beach, the turquoise ocean dazzling in the distance. A warm, citrus breeze wafts through the open windows, catching on the white cloth drapes.

It's gorgeous here. And even though I'm in enemy territory, I've never been to the coast before. A thrill bubbles up in my chest every time I taste salt on the breeze.

By the afternoon, my muscles burn from all the cleaning, but it's a good burn. It says: I did something today. I moved, I lived, I conquered.

As I wander the halls, I snag a peony from a vase of flowers and tuck it in the buttonhole of my overalls. It's a nice little 'fuck you' to them all.

Through the day, other staff have been cropping up through the house and gardens, their presence making me jump. A team of three men prune a row of apple trees, with wicker baskets groaning full of apples at their feet. A window washer soaps and sprays the pool house and conservatory, and an older man and woman bring fresh groceries and a basket of Italian wines.

They're all friendly enough, nodding and smiling, but it quickly becomes clear that we are not a *team*. The agency hires us to do our separate jobs, and we turn up and do them. Then everyone else drives back the way they came, and I'm the schmuck who's stuck here.

Once the evening shadows lengthen on the grass, a man pulls into the driveway in a white chef's uniform. I watch from the open plan living-room-slash-kitchen, holding a watering can over the windowsill herbs.

Um: hello. This guy is *cute*. He ruffles his messy brown curls and pushes his glasses up his nose as he hurries up to the house in a whirl of energy.

"Aha!" he shouts when he bursts into the kitchen and sees

me drowning the plants. "People."

"Uh." You'd think the Birchwood boys would have traumatized me for life by now, but a traitorous grin breaks over my face. "Hi. I'm Layla, the maid."

"Hello, Layla Maid."

The man makes a beeline to the kitchen before slapping a folder down on the counter top. He pages through the folder, glancing up at me and rewarding my grin with a flash of the most delicious dimple.

"Are you the chef?" I ask stupidly, because apparently dimples make me a fucking clown.

"I'm…" The man frowns at his folder, then squints up at me. "What day is it?"

I swallow a laugh. "Sunday."

"Yes, of course. Sunday." He nods furiously, paging back through the folder in the opposite direction. "I'm Diego," he offers as he flicks through, shooting me another megawatt smile. "Chef du jour. Chef of every jour."

I *giggle.* I can't help it. After Eli and his cronies with their glares and muttered insults, talking to Diego feels like I've just sucked on a helium balloon. My head is practically bouncing off the cavernous ceiling, I feel so light.

Diego slams two fingers down on one page, bending down and squinting to read it even with his glasses. Then he's off, whirling around the kitchen, banging pots and grabbing utensils.

"Do you want a hand?"

I'm hardly a sous-chef, but I'll take any excuse to linger around this bright, handsome man. Diego glances over then slams to a halt. He rakes his eyes over my overalls and bare feet and wrinkles his nose.

"Oh honey, what have they done to you?"

For a second, I'm stunned. Not because a sexy chef called me out on my clothes, but because someone has finally given me the benefit of the doubt. Moisture wells up in my eyes and I blink it away, inwardly cursing my body's need to cry at every damn emotion.

"You know the guests?"

I guess it's possible the guys aren't solely fucking with me and have been here before. But I know for a fact they went to Colorado last year.

I hate that they were on my radar like that, back before they turned on me. I hate that I used to watch them walking together across the quad and wish I could slot in between them.

Diego snorts. "No, honey. But one rich asshole is the same as another, don't you think?"

Oh, hell yeah. I know right in this moment that Diego and I will get along just fine.

"They locked me out of my room. My uniform, my shoes, my phone — it's all in my bedroom." I pause, not sure how much to tell him. Whether he'll report me to the agency. "I know them from college. We... kind of have a bet going. Forty thousand dollars if I last through the summer."

Diego pauses in his manic whirl around the kitchen, a mystery smear already on the lens of his glasses.

"That's a lot of money, Layla Maid. For that kind of sum, they must really want to hurt you."

I shrug. This is not news to me. Making a profit off their spite, though—that's new.

Diego lingers, holding a whisk in one hand and a knife in the other, before clattering it all down on the counter. Tapping his nose, he bolts out of the kitchen, his footsteps echoing across the lobby. Through the window, I watch him jog to his car, fumble in the glove compartment, then run back to the house.

Apparently, Diego only functions at a hundred miles-per-hour. I love it.

"Here." He presses a key into my palm, then scrubs his hands in the sink. "It's a skeleton key. It opens every door in this house. I made the agency give me one last year. The idiot maid kept locking me out of the pantry." He shoots me an awkward grin. "Sorry."

I turn the key over in my palm. It's just a spindly silver key with a serrated edge, but I close my fist and squeeze it tight.

"This idiot maid is thrilled. You're a God-send, Diego." My throat is suddenly tight, but I force the words out. "Thank you. These guys have it out for me. You might have just saved my skin."

Diego gives me a sad smile, his lips curling down, but I don't detect any pity. And why would he feel sorry for me? I took that damn bet.

His stillness doesn't last for long: Diego's all business, slapping vegetables and herbs and four whole fresh fish onto separate chopping boards.

"These rich boys and their vicious little games." He slices into a fish with a boning knife. "Give them hell, Layla Maid."

Chapter 4

For the next few days, I keep my head down and stay away from the Birchwood boys. That Sunday evening, Eli frowned when he came to taunt me about being locked out and found me already in my room. I beamed up at him, cross-legged on the floor and sewing a cactus decal onto my jacket in honor of Calvin. That rankled him even more, but he tapped on the door frame and wandered off again.

Good. Let him wonder. My skeleton key now spends every day safely dangling from a cord around my neck. No way is he catching me out like that twice.

Even without the bet, working as a live-in maid is harder than I thought. I guess I didn't realize how draining it would be to be on call twenty-four-seven. I've had plenty of cleaning and service jobs before, but I've always been able to clock off and get back to my own life.

Not with this job. I guess that's why it's paying next semester's rent.

The Birchwood boys are more house-trained than I expected, considering they've come all this way to make me miserable. I keep bracing to find mounds of garbage in the living room, or rodents let loose indoors.

Nope. So far... they've been pretty tame. I guess they want

to live in a trash heap less than they want me to clean one.

That doesn't mean they're not laying traps. On Monday, I find three separate wallets abandoned on desks and coffee tables. Each time, I pause and stare at the wallet, edging closer like it might bite.

I'm supposed to pick up after them. It's literally what I'm paid for. And that includes their personal stuff, right? Except I know without a doubt that the second my fingerprints touch that leather, I'll be out on my ass with allegations of theft to my name.

Knowing Eli, I won't just be fired: I'll be carted away in the back of a cop car.

But refusing to pick up their personal crap goes directly against agency policy.

I compromise, leaving passive-aggressive post-it notes on their kitchen fridge. I write in a cheery, looping script: 'Someone's wallet is on the library table!!', with two exclamation points because I know that gives Jasper a migraine.

Diego snorts when he sees the notes, digging out a sharpie and adding a smiley face to each.

"I hope this isn't their idea of a challenge. My abuela wouldn't fall for this crap."

I'm so glad he's here. He anchors me, reminds me that there are decent people out there and the Birchwood boys aren't the norm. I time my living room clean with his arrival each day, so we can hijack the sound system and dance as we work.

I blast angry girl-pop playlists, because I *know* it will make Nate's ears bleed.

Eli barges in on our dance party on Tuesday evening. I'm balanced on a chair, stretching to dust the corners of the window frame and shaking my ass in my maid outfit. He

43

takes one look at me and practically spits on the rug, storming over to shut off the sound system.

"That's enough of that, I think."

His tone is light, but he's practically vibrating on the spot. I've struck gold here—I wasn't even trying that hard to mess with them. Dancing while I clean is just more fun.

I hop down off my chair, a grin plastered over my face.

"You should try it, Henderson. That stick might finally fall out of your ass."

I sashay over and slap the music back on, dialing up the volume for good measure. Diego whoops from the kitchen, shimmying as he ladles stock into his risotto, and I toss my head back and laugh.

Eli grips my elbow hard and leans into my shoulder.

"You're making it pretty fucking easy to get you fired."

I shrug and sway my hips to the beat, reaching up to toy with Eli's open collar. "You could get me fired whenever you like. The agency won't give a shit; we both know that. But that's not why you want me here, is it Eli? You want to *break* me, remember?"

He smacks my hand away, glaring down at my swaying hips with disgust. I'm playing with fire, taunting him like this. He's gone weirdly easy on me for the first few days—probably to lull me into a false sense of security.

The glimmer of loathing in his eyes tells me my peace is about to shatter.

Fuck it. I knew full well what they're capable of when I accepted the bet. I've been meek for so long, taking what they dished out on campus and giving nothing back.

They want to do this properly? Bring it on.

I won't sit there and not mess with them in return.

* * *

Case in point: watching Jasper find those notes on the fridge. It's small, but so fucking satisfying. Jasper has a *thing,* some mental tic about proper grammar and punctuation. Misplaced apostrophes make him *squirm.* I noticed his quirk in a tutorial group in first year, and back then I thought it was oh-so-fucking-adorable.

I don't find it cute anymore. I find it useful. A weakness to exploit.

Jasper comes into the kitchen one morning while I'm shoulder-deep in the oven, scrubbing at the sides. He doesn't deign to glance at me, stepping over my bare legs like I'm part of the furniture. Clad in a purple button-down shirt and gray chinos, he seriously has me wondering if any of these guys know how to relax.

He grips the fridge handle and pauses, eyes narrowing as he takes in the notes. I watch, gleeful, as his shoulders creep towards his ears. His cheeks flush red and I swear his eye twitches.

Then he's snatching the notes down and crumpling them into a ball. "Very clever," he mutters as he tosses them in the garbage.

His voice is tight, like I've physically pained him. Perfect.

When he wrenches the fridge open, the jars lining the shelves rattle against each other.

They're minor acts of rebellion—if they're keeping things tame, I'm sure as hell not going to be the one to escalate. But they add steel to my spine in all those moments when the Birchwood boys look at me like some kind of invasive insect. Which, you know, is pretty much any time I walk into a room.

I've survived a full year of their torment already. They'll need to try harder than a few dirty looks and weak pranks to break me now.

* * *

Okay, so I got cocky. I thought they'd gone soft.

I guess they really were just biding their time.

The day after Eli crashes our dance party, I go back to my annex at dinner and find my bedroom empty. My laptop is gone from my writing desk; my closet door hangs open, displaying empty hangers. My bed has no quilt; my bedside cabinet is bare. The books that were here before I arrived are missing from their shelf. Even Calvin is gone.

Right. Stealing my shit. Real original.

I keep a serene calm pasted on my face as I wander the halls, checking each of the mansion rooms, but the guys snicker when they see me looking.

Whatever. If they fucked Calvin up somehow, I'll make them pay.

I check the guest rooms, the cupboards, the pantry. The flowerbeds and the maze. My teeth grit harder and harder as I search, my heart pounding sickly in my chest.

It's just stuff, I tell myself over and over. *You win the bet and you can replace it and more.*

Finally, after hours of searching, I find everything I own floating in the pool.

Well, not *everything*. I'm not a complete idiot. The first day I arrived, I inspected every inch of my room until I found a loose floorboard under my bed. My phone's in there, with my ID and money.

But my stashed valuables aren't the only survivors. Calvin sits in his pot on a sun lounger.

And maybe it's the sight of that little cactus unharmed, but my serene expression becomes real.

These clothes are mostly thrift store finds. The uniforms? I could give less of a shit. I fish them all out one-by-one with a long net, dropping them with a wet slap on the tiles.

I'll throw them in the laundry before bed. If I stink of chlorine for a week, it's their fault.

The laptop is more of a blow. It's sunk, a shadow on the bottom of the pool. No way that's fucking fixable. Any hope of getting ahead on assignments—hell, of catching up on Netflix over the summer—is long gone.

I chew on my nail, debating whether I should jump in and rescue the corpse.

In the end, I leave it. It'll be a nice memento for them to swim over. A reminder of how much they suck ass. And if it leaches some toxic chemical into the water, well, that's a bonus.

Every piece-of-shit prank they pull on me, I weather with a smile on my face. And every time I refuse to break, they ramp it up a notch.

They push Gertie into an ornamental gazebo and let out the tires.

I wink at Nate and call a tow truck.

They slash the skirt of my maid uniforms.

I raise the hem and flash my thigh tattoo.

What they don't realize—what they haven't noticed yet—is they've already pushed me too far. The second they followed me here, ruining my one chance for a break, for a summer without their malevolence—I officially ran out of shits to give.

They've already driven me to rock bottom.
Now I just need to cash in.

Chapter 5

The employee manual is crystal clear: the house facilities are for the guests' exclusive use. As the sole live-in staff member, I get use of the annex, and of course we all get the awesome privilege of cleaning or pruning or cooking in the main house and gardens.

On the sixth day, Pierce sends me a selfie from her family's pool house. She's sat on the pool steps, long legs crossed in the water, with a flurry of little kids splashing about in the shallow end. There's a half-sagging inflatable dinosaur floating past, for God's sake.

I need in.

As far as I can tell, none of these assholes have even stepped foot in the pool house except to trash my things. I go in there to 'clean', just in case, frowning sadly down at the shadow of my laptop, but the fluffy white towels are all stacked on the shelves undisturbed.

Fuck it. Operation Summer Vacation is go.

I scope it out for a few days, and wait until gone midnight to be sure. The annex has its own back door which opens onto the gardens, and I let myself out to the paved path before nudging the door shut. The skeleton key dangles under my sweatshirt, a reassuring weight against my collarbone.

The windows of the house are dark, at least on this side. If the Birchwood boys are up, they're staying far away from the staff quarters.

That is just fine with me.

I tiptoe down the path, flip flops tapping against the stone. The night air is warm, laced with jasmine, and for a crazy moment I'm back in Santa Fe, sneaking out to stargaze on a school night. The memory fills me up and I take in the stars, bright pinpricks in the inky black overhead.

I love the stars. They make me feel small and big at the same time. Like I'm just one girl in an infinite universe of people and creatures and mysteries, but I'm also my own tiny galaxy of atoms, rooted in this exact space and time.

Eli would have a field day if I told him something like that.

Doesn't matter. We're not exactly pen pals.

I hug my towel to my chest and follow the winding path through the flowerbeds, tripping over my own feet when I can't drag my eyes away from the sky.

The pool house is shadowed and empty. Kind of eerie, alone at night. The thump of the door echoes through the silent, cavernous space, and then all I can hear is my own breathing. The water laps against the tiles, tinted silver in the moonlight spilling through the glass walls.

My sweatshirt and joggers whisper against my skin as I pull them off. They fall in a pile with my flip-flops and towel, then the only thing between me and the humid air is my skimpy bikini. It's a watermelon print—a gift from Pierce when we got our jobs offers and heard the ocean calling our names.

Ah, Past Layla. That clueless fool. I owe her this.

I haven't even seen the beach yet. I don't know what's stopping me, but every time I duck out of the annex for a late night walk, I wheel around and wander the gardens instead.

I can still hear the ocean, though, if I listen hard from the grounds. The gentle *hush, hush* of the waves.

Baby steps. A pool is a good place to start. I'll swim here first, get some practice in—we didn't exactly swim much back in Santa Fe. Then before I know it, I'll be out there on the beach, soaring across the waves on a surfboard.

A girl can dream, right?

The water is cooler than I expect. I inch down the carved stone steps, goosebumps prickling over my skin as cold water licks at my legs. My nipples tighten beneath the triangles of my bikini, and I huff out a hard breath.

A flash of movement through the glass has me plunging into the water. I lurch forward, ripples spreading out from me, and crane my neck to scan the gardens. The trees and paths are silent, the fountain switched off for the night.

My racing heartbeat slows, and I drift towards the deep end. There are owls roosting on the property; I hear them at night sometimes. That flash was probably an owl swooping for a mouse.

The shadows are thicker at the deep end of the pool, where even the moonlight can't reach. I'm clinging to the side of the pool to catch my breath when the door creaks open.

Shit. I sink down to my chin, pressing into the tiled corner.

A dark figure pads into the pool house as fear snakes through my gut. It must be a Birchwood boy—the figure is tall, with broad shoulders—and he moves straight past the light switches to the edge of the pool. My heart hammers against my rib cage, so hard I'm surprised he can't hear it, and I edge towards the steps as quick as I can without sloshing the water.

The man stops at the pile of my clothes. He prods them with

his foot, then he scans the pool for me. Maddox Landry steps into the moonlight, frustration etched in his face.

"I didn't think you'd dare to come in here." He doesn't raise his voice—he doesn't have to. It bounces off the walls and tickles at the back of my neck. He keeps scanning as he speaks, and I realize he hasn't seen me yet.

The relief I feel is short-lived. What am I going to do, teleport myself out of the pool and back into my clothes?

I push off the wall and his head snaps in my direction. I drift into the patch of moonlight. "I thought you were all asleep."

Maddox Landry looks different at night. He looks… softer. In the harsh light of day, he's all tight black t-shirts and rings on his fingers and a turned-down mouth. Right now he's bundled in a zip-up hoodie and sweatpants, his brown hair mussed like he's been tossing and turning.

I wonder if Maddox is truly half as calm as he seems.

"You thought wrong."

Right. He may look rumpled and sweet, but Maddox Landry is just as much a dick as his friends.

I breast-stroke towards the steps with as much dignity as I can muster. With my head held high above the water, my pony tail drags behind me and swirls around my shoulders.

"I'll get out of your hair, *sir*."

Maddox scoffs and paces to the glass wall and back.

"You don't have to do that," he grits out as I stand up in the shallow end. The water laps at my thighs, and even in the dark I can tell Maddox is staring at my watermelon bikini. "You can stay."

A smirk spreads across my face and I swirl my hands in the water.

"Just don't fucking bother me," he adds, and my smirk

evaporates.

The water cradles me, lifting my limbs as I sit back and watch Maddox change. He pulls his hoodie and t-shirt off in one motion, then hesitates with his thumbs hooked in the waistband of his sweatpants. With a sigh, he pushes those down too, until he's stood in only his boxers.

They're black with little white crescent moons. My stomach swoops.

"Did you come here to skinny dip, Maddox?" I tease, forgetting for a second that he hates me. He must forget too, because even though he shakes his head, there's a smile tugging at his lips.

"You're just lucky I noticed you were here."

"Or unlucky," I blurt.

Damn it. Maddox falls silent, and my mind goes horribly blank. I need to say something, need to break the tension growing between us.

"It's always better when you assholes don't notice me," I manage at last, though my voice comes out strangled.

Maddox grunts and walks to the deep end, the moonlight catching on his sculpted chest like a Greek statue come to life. "Don't bother me and I won't bother you," he says, and dives into the pool.

It's not the night I had planned, and I hover there for a full minute, but eventually I drift to the far side of the pool.

It's kind of restful swimming laps with Maddox Landry. He swims about three lengths for every one of mine, powerful arms cleaving through the water and propelling him forwards with barely a splash. I'm a terrier at a duck pond in comparison, but I force the self-consciousness down—*who gives a shit what he thinks, Layla*—and focus on the sweet burn in my limbs.

Part way through, Maddox stops to catch his breath and mutters about his hair getting in his eyes. I cling to the side, warring with myself, before pushing off and swimming over.

I give him the spare hair band from my wrist, and he scrapes his wet hair back in a bun.

It's almost pleasant.

After an hour or so, we both get out by unspoken agreement. We towel off in silence, slipping our clothes on over our wet things and wringing out our hair.

"Thank you," Maddox murmurs, his mouth turned down like he's disappointed with himself. He holds out my hair band.

My poor heart. In the quiet of the pool house, he can probably hear the way my breath shakes as I draw it into my lungs.

"Keep it." I can't believe I'm saying this. "For next time."

He nods, and then he's out the door, slipping into the shadows of the gardens. I stay put, toes scrunching in my flip-flops, inhaling the scent of chlorine and trying to kid myself that I hate Maddox Landry.

* * *

My dreamy mood from my midnight swim is short-lived. The next day, I wake up late, thighs tangled in my sheets. The day goes downhill from there.

I'm running too far behind for breakfast, and by the time I can finally sneak a break mid-morning, my stomach is clenching on nothing and my fingers tremble. I take a risk, grabbing a coffee from the main kitchen's fancy coffee machine, and when I lift the steaming mug to my lips, a voice startles it right out of my hands.

"Stealing from our kitchen?"

Jasper strolls through the doorway, hands in his pockets. He's in a t-shirt for once, the white cotton stretching over his surprisingly broad chest. He's not as built as Nate or Maddox, and he's stretched taller than Eli, but his shoulders are markedly wider than his hips.

Jasper tosses a smirk over his shoulder. "Let's remind the agency to dock her wages."

Nate prowls in behind him, a tank top and sweatpants clinging to his tattooed frame. They've been for a run together, with cheeks flushed and sweat slicking their skin.

Ugh, whatever. Forty thousand dollars, baby.

Nate glares, catching my side-eye, and heat crawls up my neck. I jerk around and dig through the cupboards for a cloth to soak up the steaming puddle on the tiles. Shards of ceramic mug tinkle as I scrape them into a dustpan.

"Some fucking maid." Nate's voice always sounds harsh, even with his friends, but he seems to keep an extra bite just for me. "She leaves more mess than she finds."

I roll my eyes, mopping up the last of the coffee. It's a stupid dig: they know I keep this house spotless.

"Something tells me she wasn't hired for her cleaning skills," Jasper leers, and I glare at him for that. He meets me straight on, his flushed face intense.

I tug at my shortened dress, regretting that payback.

They bitch together about the state of me, about how I'm gagging for it, and I roll my eyes and scrub the counter tops. Truthfully, every surface in here is clean enough to eat off—I wiped the kitchen down ten minutes ago. But I won't let these assholes think they have me running rattled.

"Tell me, *Layla Maid*," Jasper says, my playful nickname from

Diego scathing in his mouth. He leans one hip against the counter next to me, and I inch away before Nate jumps up to sit on my other side.

Sweat prickles across my lower back, but I keep scrubbing.

"How does it feel to be in the same house as Eli? Do you get wet when he walks in a room?"

"She's a stalker." Nate swipes a green apple from the fruit bowl and takes a bite. "She probably sneaks into his room when we're gone to sniff his boxers."

He leans close, the thin chain he wears around his neck lifting away from his collarbone. "Does it make you hopeful? Being so near? Do you think if you pant and moan loud enough from your shitty little annex that he'll forget what you did last time and come running?"

I pause the sponge, pressing it flat to the marble. When I look up at Nate, his face is inches above mine; his warm breath gusts over my neck.

"It makes me jealous. Being here with him. With you." Nate's lip curls up in a snarl, but I'm not done yet.

"I look at every mansion along this beach, every single house filled with bankers and mobsters and billionaires. People who ruin lives and smile while they do it. And I am sick-to-my-stomach jealous that I'm stuck here with you four."

Nate sneers, but I push away from the counter and walk to the doorway. I force myself to take slow, even steps, so they don't see the way my chest heaves and my legs tremble. When I reach the large, arching doorway, I spin around and tell them one more thing.

"I wanted Eli once, it's true, but that's before I really knew him. You know what I think of the four of you now?"

Jasper crosses his arms and Nate cocks his head. Their faces are imperious, and my hands ball into fists.

"I'd rather die than touch any single one of you."

Chapter 6

E li's palms are warm and dry, skating over the bare skin of my arms, my neck, my back. He cradles my jaw and tips my head away, leaning over me to whisper against my lips.

"Fuck, Layla. I've never—you make me—fucking hell."

I lunge forward, pressing my mouth against his. I've dreamed about this moment for so long, every single day since our fingers brushed in the library and shivers skated up my arm. After months of stolen glances and secret smiles, of nerves churning my stomach whenever he so much as looks at me, Eli Henderson and I are alone.

The thumping bass of the party bleeds through the cracks around the door, but in here we're in our own world. Eli presses me deeper into the tangle of coats lining the wall, and I pull him with me by the belt loops. Now that we're finally touching, skin to skin, hip to hip, every split second apart feels like torture. I grasp for him like I'm making up for lost time, and he pays me back tenfold.

"Eli." I tear my lips away and he ducks down to suck at my throat. "That'll leave a mark," I laugh weakly, and his teeth scrape my skin.

"Good."

The cloakroom is dark, the sounds of the revelers beyond the door muffled, and it makes me bold. I slide one palm down his chest, the buttons of his shirt catching on my fingertips. It's harder than I'd *thought to undo his belt, and I fumble in the cage of his arms. The drink spins my head, but I'm a good kind of tipsy. Unfettered and soaring.*

"We should go somewhere else, somewhere private," Eli mutters, his voice rough. "People might come in."

But he doesn't stop my clumsy fingers. He stands there, chest heaving so hard it brushes against mine, while I work his belt open and start in on his pants.

"Please," I breathe into his mouth, pausing to suck on his tongue. He groans and it vibrates through me, rattling my bones. "Please, Eli. I need you."

If we were in daylight, if I were sober, I'd choke on those words and flush dark red with embarrassment. But here with Eli, tucked away secret and safe, I'm not ashamed.

I'm powerful. Hungry.

With every kiss, every press of his body to mine, raw energy fills me until I'm smoldering with it. Eli's lips capture mine again and his kiss is biting, fierce. He molds our bodies together and thrusts his hips into mine.

"Yeah." Teeth nibble at my earlobe and strong fingers slide under my shirt. "Fuck. Layla. I need you too."

* * *

I blink my eyes open, forehead resting against the wall. I lurch backwards, away from the empty coat hooks that line the beach house cloakroom.

My heart thunders like I've gone for a run, not drifted off in a closet and let memories consume me.

I haven't thought about that night in months. I don't let myself. It brings a bitter taste to my mouth, and even worse, it makes me ache.

But the Birchwood boys have been working me to exhaustion, dragging me out of bed at all hours for the pettiest reasons: to wash a single plate, mop up a tiny spill.

I've barely kept my eyes open all morning. It must have finally pulled me under—and in this room of all places.

My scattered cleaning supplies trip me and crumple under my feet as I stagger to the doorway. The pale blue walls of the cloakroom are close, too close, and I need air.

I need to get far away from here; to shake off the memories that cling to me like cobwebs.

I burst out of the cloakroom, sucking in a huge breath, and Eli pauses at the foot of the stairs. He frowns at me, phone gripped in one hand, but I don't have time for whatever snide remark he's about to throw at me.

I lunge through the front door and out onto the driveway. The scent of freshly cut grass is strong in the air, strong enough to taste, and I work on taking big, slow breaths as I plunge into the gardens. The last thing I need is Eli Henderson or one of the other Birchwood boys seeing me like this. They make an Olympic sport out of kicking me when I'm down.

"Layla Maid?"

A strangled sob works its way out my throat, and I'm about to take off running when a gentle hand takes my elbow. Diego stares down at me, eyes wide behind his glasses.

"What happened? Did they hurt you?"

His grip tightens on my arm and he glares at the living room window. I follow his gaze and flinch when I see Eli lounging against the glass, arms crossed as he watches us.

Diego swears under his breath before placing his hands on my shoulders. "It's going to be okay, honey. You tell me which one hurt you and I'll deal with it."

From the acid in his voice, I know that Diego's version of 'dealing with it' will be bloody. I shake my head, because no way am I letting him put his job on the line for me. Not over a stupid panic attack.

"They didn't hurt me." No more than usual, anyway. And for once, they didn't even know they were doing it. "I just... I was cleaning, and it was like the walls were closing in on me."

I try for a reassuring smile, but it feels lopsided. "I guess the bleach fumes got to me."

Diego drags his eyes over my face, then over my body for good measure. It's not like when Eli or Nate or even the other guys look at me. It's careful, concerned. Warmth spreads through my shaky limbs, and I feel stronger already.

"What a dumb thing to freak out over." I give a shaky laugh, but it's genuine this time. Diego's mouth quirks and he lets go of my shoulders. I can't help it: I steal a glance at where Eli stood, but the living room is empty.

"It's not dumb. Bleach fumes are no joke, Layla Maid."

I laugh. "I should ask for hazard pay."

We stroll down the path together, my fingers stroking over the rose bushes. I like the soft brush of the petals and the sharp prick of thorns. Their scent wafts over us, my pulse finally slowing.

Right on cue, my stomach rumbles. Lunch time. After missing breakfast and then dropping my stolen coffee, it's a wonder I'm not more of a wreck.

"Wait, why are you here so early?"

Diego comes every evening to prepare dinner; for their other meals, the guys fend for themselves.

Diego scoffs and shoves his hands in the pockets of his chef uniform. "These parties don't come together in an hour, honey. I'll be here all day, right until the guests arrive."

Uh. What?

My confusion must show on my face, because Diego raises his eyebrows.

"They didn't tell you?"

I huff and swipe the rosebushes harder than necessary. A rosebud tumbles off its stalk and drops onto the path.

"No. They didn't tell me."

Because why would they? Assholes. Diego grumbles under his breath, then clasps my shoulder as we walk.

"Don't let it bother you, Layla Maid. They can't hurt you where it counts."

They already have, I think to myself, but I shut that down. Diego's right: maybe they hurt me like that once, but they never will again.

That would require that I trust them. They can't betray me if I keep them at arm's length.

We round the corner and pass Maddox and Nate sprawled in the grass. I've swum with Maddox a couple more times since that first night, our interactions cool but polite. It's a balm. A reprieve. When we step into that shadowed pool house, we're stepping out of reality.

He's still a prick in the daylight, though. It's worse now that my traitorous cheeks blush whenever I see him. He's bent over a paperback, while Nate lies with a forearm tossed over his face.

I clear my throat and stare straight ahead at the path. Diego leans into my shoulder, waving at Maddox as he whispers in my ear.

"I'll hide some treats away for you. These assholes will be

gunning for you tonight."

* * *

In the space of a day, the beach-side mansion and its gardens transform into a hedonistic fairy glade. Lanterns dangle through the trees and the maze, and pop-up bars spring up through the house and grounds. Dark satin drapes cover the walls and oil paintings, and in most rooms the staff clear all furniture except for velvet-clad fainting couches.

Glass flutes and tumblers line every available surface, sparkling clean and ready for drinks. After lunch, I watched the alcohol delivery arrive: crate after crate of expensive bottles wheeled up the driveway.

There are enough spirits in this house that one stray match could send it up in flames. I got a preemptive, second-hand hangover just watching those bars stock up.

The Birchwood boys never give me a heads-up about the party. I guess if they got their way, I wouldn't notice any of the preparations, and I'd be completely blindsided.

Thank God I have Diego. Oh, and I'm not fucking blind.

When the first guests arrive, their laughter bouncing down the driveway, I stand in front of my bedroom mirror and smooth the creases out of my maid uniform. It's a formal party, judging by the setup, but at least the agency has a stick up its ass about uniforms. My dress isn't fancy by any means, but at least I won't stick out as the resident slob.

I pull my hair into a high ponytail and slick on blood-red lipstick. Breathe in, breathe out. It's just a party; a job; a crowd of mini-bankers and wannabe politicians.

I tip my chin up and straighten my spine.

Get out there, Layla.

There's no awkward early stage like in most parties, loitering with a handful of guests in the lobby. No: the house goes from virtually empty to bustling in the space of a few minutes. Everywhere I look, there are men in sleek suits and women in cocktail dresses. And all of them wear an ornate mask on their face.

They're young—that's what jars me the most. Even with the masks blocking their eyes, their noses, I can tell they're all in their twenties.

But they're a whole other species from the average college student—from *me*. These people may be young, but power and wealth crackles through the air around them. They're the ruling class; their parents hold their world in their palms, and one day soon, these people will inherit it.

Naturally, they're pricks. They sneer at the waiters and grope for the waitresses. The women give each other catty smiles, then roll their eyes as soon as backs are turned.

Someone has cranked the sound system loud enough to thrum through the walls: dark, throbbing beats which stir the satin drapes. Agency waitresses wind their ways through the crowd, platters of canapes held aloft on silver trays.

And I realize with a jolt that the other staff all have masks. Matching black satin masks with embroidered detailing.

Mine is the only naked face on the grounds.

I'm surrounded. The crowd is everywhere. They're packed into the rooms like sardines, laughing and grasping each other to the music. They're spilling out into the gardens, the pool house doors thrown wide to the night air. All of them, reveling in their decadent anonymity—and smirking at my bare, blushing face.

Designer dresses snag on my uniform as I brush past. A drink splatters down my back. So many stilettos step on my toes that after an hour I change into my Docs. While I'm safe in my room, I consider trying to fashion some kind of face covering from my clothes, but decide against it.

I don't want the Birchwood boys to know they've rattled me.

I double-check the lock on my annex doors before I leave. No way do I want rich, premarital babies made on my patchwork bedspread.

If there's one guarantee in life, it's that plying a crowd with alcohol means hands start to wander. I grit my teeth and dodge as best I can, throwing out my elbows when the rowdier guests don't get the picture. Their refined grace soon falls away with the drink, and they become sloppy. Feral. More like the Greek parties on campus—like the new-grown adults they are.

"Hey, Nate!" One of them yells when I have to shove him off with my shoulder. Across the library at the makeshift bar, a crimson mask with a curved black beak looks over. "Why is the help such a fucking prude?"

The crimson mask glances between us, from the swaying guy sweating through his tuxedo to my flushed grimace.

I hate that Nate can see my face. Can see what tonight is doing to me. The crimson mask cocks to one side, like the bird it's modeled after.

"Don't take it personally, man," Nate calls, loud enough that nearby guests glance over too.

Perfect. I'm a creature in a zoo.

"Layla Maid is only open for business to the rich and famous."

I twist my mouth, bitterness sour on my tongue. But what did I expect? Nate goes back to directing the bartender to mix some ungodly cocktail, and the guest leers down at me through his forest-green mask, reaching out to skate his thumb over my hemline.

"If rich is what you need, baby, my family's all set. I'll slip you a grand in cash right now to take a walk in the gardens."

Take a walk. Yeah, right. Fucking Nate Becker.

I lean in close, like I'm tempted, reaching up to run a finger over the edge of his mask. Then I shove my knee in his balls and tear it off his face, so I can see exactly who propositioned me.

He's bright red and spluttering, eyes glassy and dilated. Brown hair flops over his forehead. He chokes and doubles over, sloshing his drink over the front of my dress, and I hear Nate whooping in the background.

Anyone. He could be anyone. And really, who fucking cares?

I won this round, anyway: I have a mask. I slip it on as I leave, pulling the elastic tighter, the cheek and nose hollows way too big and slipping down my face. It stinks of sweat, the inside damp, but my heart slows with relief.

I'm hidden, like everyone else. I'm safe.

I go to leave, but a figure lounges against the door frame, blocking the way so I have to squeeze past. Below a dove gray mask crusted with pearls, a mouth that is unmistakably Maddox's opens to speak.

I hold up a hand, pausing shoulder-to-shoulder.

"Complain to the agency and I'll report you all for pimping me out."

The slide of my too-big mask down my nose ruins my harsh tone. But his mouth slams shut, and I barge past, elbowing my way to the hall.

Fucking rich people. They start the night so snooty and refined, and they end it throwing up in a plant pot just like everyone else.

I step over slumped bodies and outstretched legs, trying not to think about the clean-up tomorrow. My boot catches on an abandoned pint glass, shattering the glass and sending sticky amber liquid flooding down the stairs.

Fuck, I hate parties.

The Birchwood boys deserve a little retribution, so I slip between the crowds and the wall and dart to their rooms. Jasper's is the first one I reach: I jiggle the doorknob. Locked.

Well, it might have stayed that way if they weren't such massive pricks. It's the work of a second to slip my skeleton key from around my neck and twist the lock open. Drunken party-goers are already whooping and spilling into the bedroom before I turn my back.

Maddox's room is next. Then Nate's. Then Eli's.

Let's see how they like their party now.

The crowd's a little thinner as I head downstairs to the lobby, and I lean against a wall to catch my breath. I wish I knew the damn time, but I locked all my valuables in my bedroom and there's no way I'm hunting for a clock. Judging by the bright eyes and raucous laughter, tonight will go on for a while yet.

"Fancy seeing you here."

A smooth voice startles me away from the wall. Eli lounges against the cloakroom doorway, lips twisted in a smirk below a midnight blue mask. I'd know those piercing blue eyes and the curl of his dark hair anywhere. Hell, I know the shape of his *shoulders* by heart.

"Have we met?" I say anyway.

"Oh, Layla." His soft mouth quirks up on one side. "We're *intimately* acquainted, as you well know."

I sigh, my damp dress sticky against my skin. "What do you

want, Eli?"

He doesn't tell me. That would be too easy. No: he gives me another predatory smile and turns to lean against his shoulder.

"So many happy memories," he says, tapping the cloakroom door frame, and I hate that he does this. I hate that he takes the most vulnerable, passionate moments of my life and twists them into a sick joke.

I grit my teeth, grateful that the mask hides so much of my face.

"For you, maybe."

Oh, Eli does not like that. Rage flickers across his eyes.

"Let's reminisce, shall we?"

He takes my wrist before I can react and pulls me into the cloakroom, snapping at a moaning couple in the corner to get the hell out. Once we're alone in the dark, he nudges me back into the coats, hands braced on my shoulders.

"Perfect," he breathes. "A little trip down memory lane."

I close my eyes. Emptiness yawns wide in my chest, like my ribs are crumpling in on themselves.

"Now, what did you say that night, Layla?" He snaps his fingers. "That's right. You said you needed it."

Eli slides his thigh between my legs and grips my waist hard.

"Do you still need it, Layla? Do you want to rub against me, get yourself off on my thigh?"

Traitorous heat blooms in my core even as tears brim behind my eyelids.

"No," I choke. Eli's leg moves away, but his hands stay on my waist. I gather myself to my full height, my ponytail dragging through the thick mass of coats. "I'd rather be the whore you say I am than ever touch you again."

I gather what's left of my strength and shove him back with

shaky arms. When I wrench the door open, light spills into the cloakroom.

"I'm done for the night," I croak, and Eli doesn't argue. "Find some other girl to torture."

Tears slide down my cheeks behind my mask as I fight my way back to the annex. Some guests try to call for me, waving empty glasses, but I don't care. And when Jasper spots me from the kitchen, his mask shoved up onto his forehead, he frowns for all of half a minute before turning back to the girl pressed against the fridge.

Let them swig their spirits and fuck random girls and party themselves into a coma.

I don't care. I won't care.

The Birchwood boys are nothing to me.

They broke into my annex because of course they fucking did. Empty bottles and pools of spilled drinks cover the tiles. My kitchen cupboards have been raided, all of my carefully budgeted snacks for the week stolen. They even ravaged the secret plate of canapes that Diego left for me.

"Bunch of animals," I grumble to myself, grabbing a broom and going from room to room to evict the squatters.

"It's a fucking party, chill," one girl says as she disentangles herself from a sloppy drunk in a rumpled suit.

"Take your trash with you, please," I tell her, and stand over them both with the broom until she drags her date bitching and moaning all the way back to the house.

I have exactly zero fucks left to give. Especially when I find the trio rubbing their body parts all over my bedspread.

"Out!"

I slam the door open and the two girls shriek and cover their bits. All three of them are naked except for their masks. The

69

guy leans back and smirks, not trying to hide at all.

"Want to join, gorgeous?"

Jesus.

"So help me, I will stick this broom where the sun don't shine."

That has them scrambling up, snatching their clothes off the floor and cursing me out as they leave.

By the time I finish with pest control, my poor annex looks like a bomb hit. I am sticky and sweaty; tired to my very soul. I slump against my closed bedroom door, listening to the music thump through the house with gnawing despair.

"Please, please, please." I push away from the door and kneel at my bedside. Sliding onto my belly, I pry up the loose floorboard under the bed.

In the small hole, my fingertips find the corner of my wallet, my phone, my small jewelry box. I breathe out a sigh. Finally, a win.

Also under my bed, pushed far into the corner, I find a dusty bottle. The canapes might have died a tragic death, but the rest of Diego's gift is alive and well. I pull the champagne out and inspect the label: the name means nothing to me, which means it must be obscenely expensive.

The smart thing to do would be to sell it. Put the money towards next semester and pat myself on the back for being sensible.

I don't want to be smart. Taking this job was a smart move, and look where that got me.

I throw on some shorts and my sweatshirt before retying my mask—I am no one's fucking maid right now. And no way am I putting on a cheap summer dress and trying to blend in.

The Docs stay, too. I want to stamp a bitch if need be.

With the doors locked and my fizzing champagne bottle gripped by the neck, I set off into the gardens.

They want a night to be primal, to come unhinged?

Fine. I'm in.

Chapter 7

I n my limited experience, which is mostly based on TV shows, rich people gardens are often prissy and stale. They're all manicured lawns and croquet sets and shrubs clipped to look like rabbits and frogs.

These grounds aren't like that. Sure, they're cultivated—there's a plan to the layout, and there are features dotted around that scream 'upper class'. There's the fountain, obviously, large enough to currently fit around thirty drunken revelers. They're whooping and splashing, probably trying to recreate the opening credits from Friends. I want to hate them out of spite, but part of me wishes I could join in.

Besides the fountain, there are also several gazebos, an orchard, and an honest-to-God maze. They're spread through the grounds, tucked between rockeries and flowerbeds and ornamental ponds.

I like the forgotten corners the best. The parts of the grounds without any showy features, which are left to grow a bit wilder. Tangles of meadow flowers and gnarled tree trunks. Moss covered stones.

Most of the party-goers cling to the halo of light spilling from the house, milling on the grass or chasing each other shrieking through the maze. I charge through them, champagne bottle swinging in my hand. A splash fizzes over the rim and down my wrist, and I lick it up before it can reach my sleeve.

Holy shit, that's good. Crisp and not too sweet. I send a quick thanks up to the angel that is Diego.

There are lanterns spaced along the garden paths which lead away from the house, and the occasional rustle or moan marks a more intrepid couple in the shadows. I veer off the path too, squinting at the ground so I don't step in someone sticky.

One week in, I know the way by heart. I scoped out my secret spot on the second night.

It's a ten minute walk from the house; less on nights like tonight when I lengthen my stride and stamp my frustration into the ground with each step. By the time I throw myself down in the grove, my back against a huge, twisted tree, my lungs are burning and I'm slick with sweat.

"Fucking Birchwood boys," I grumble once I've caught my breath, swigging long and hard from the bottle. A trickle of champagne slides over my chin and drips down my sweatshirt.

"We're the worst, aren't we?"

I jerk and smack my head on the tree trunk.

Maddox Landry sits against a willow tree, half shrouded by the branches.

"Yes!" I prod the back of my head, wincing at a tender spot. "You definitely are."

If he's here, I need to go. Need to find somewhere else for my pity party. But there's a rustle and the shiver of leaves, and then Maddox crouches next to me and cradles my head in his hands. I sit frozen, too shocked to stop him as he tips my skull forward and probes at my new lump. He tugs the strings of my mask undone, and it drops into my lap.

"Easily startled, aren't you, Layla Maid?"

73

I glare at my knees. They're shadowed with bruises from constantly kneeling to clean up after this prick and his friends.

"That's what happens when you creep around in the dark."

Maddox hums, and I shiver at the sound. His voice is bourbon and dripping honey.

"I was here first. I'm afraid the only creep here is you."

He lets go of my head and I watch him warily, but he doesn't seem angry. His face is relaxed behind his mask, eyes crinkling at the corners like I've said something funny.

I swig from the champagne, wiping my mouth on my sleeve, then slowly hold it out to him. Maddox lowers himself to the grass, taking the bottle without a word.

"That's good stuff," he says after a mouthful. In the moonlight, his eyes slide to mine. "Almost too good, Layla Maid."

I could deny what he's implying. Tell him it was a gift. Instead, I quirk an eyebrow and hold my hand back out for the bottle.

"Consider it a tip." His fingers brush mine as he passes it back. "A bonus for emotional damages."

I'm not really joking, but Maddox's chuckle curls around me like smoke. We pass the bottle back and forth, drinking in silence, settled into the same calm as our secret swim sessions.

Maddox reaches for the bottle again, and I notice my hair band on his wrist.

"Shit."

Why am I so fucking affected by this? By seeing my little hairband beneath his broad hand? The champagne bottle is light in my grip: we've drunk two-thirds, between us. Maybe that explains the surge in my pulse, the squeeze of my heart in my chest.

Overhead, the stars pulse in the sky, and my body is floating as I climb into his lap.

"What are you doing?"

I slide Maddox's mask off and toss it to the dirt. The line that sometimes creases his forehead is back, and I smooth it out with my thumb. He sits there and lets me, his thighs rigid below mine.

"Look." I hold his own forearm up for his inspection. "You're wearing it."

"Yes. Yeah, I…" He clears his throat. "It comes in handy."

"I bet." I toy with the silky ends of his hair where they curl against his collarbone. The moonlight washes the color out of everything, but I know the chocolate brown shade by memory. I can close my eyes and summon up the exact color, right here and now.

I tell Maddox this, letting go of his hair so I can press my hands against his chest. His throat bobs as he swallows, and in my loose, floaty state, it just about drives me wild. I duck my head and slide my teeth over his throat, then press a kiss there.

His hands slide up to grip my waist, even as he growls a warning.

"If this is a trick…"

I straighten up and match Maddox's glare with my own.

"I don't trick people. I've never tricked people."

He opens his mouth to argue, but footsteps pound towards us over the path and he tips me out of his lap onto the grass.

"So much for Southern gentlemen," I mutter from my heap, and I swear his mouth twitches, but then Jasper bursts into the grove and skids to a stop.

His mask is long gone, his blond hair ruffled and sticking up in clumps. It looks like someone's been running their hands through it, twisting and gripping.

75

Jealousy thunders through my gut, and I snatch up the bottle again to take a long pull.

"It's Nate." Jasper notices me, glancing between us with a frown before pulling Maddox to his feet. "His dad called again. He picked up."

"Fuck. Where is he?"

They set off without a backwards glance, swallowed up by the shadows.

And me? I scramble back up to sit against the tree trunk, downing what's left of the champagne. The stars blur overhead, and I try not to think about soft brown hair or the feel of a hard chest beneath my palms.

* * *

I only went to a handful of parties back on campus before the Birchwood boys turned against me. Their anti-Layla campaign was swift and brutal. By October in my second year, I'd resigned myself to Friday nights in with Pierce.

Even so, I've been to enough parties to know broadly how they go. There are the first few hours, when the drinks are flowing but no one's too drunk yet; spirits are high and everyone around you is funny and beautiful. As the night wears on, people become either sloppy or sleepy. Glasses smash, fights break out. People drag each other into closets or grope each other in plain view.

Then there's the wind down. The crowds empty out, staggering to Ubers or herded away by their designated drivers. All that's left are the stragglers: those too drunk or too desperate to avoid going home to take a hint and leave.

Those are the ones I wade through on the way back to my

room. I sat in my grove for hours, burrowed in my sweatshirt and slowly sobering up as I watched the stars.

It's not like I could just call it a night and turn in. The music blared loud enough to reach me across the grounds, and besides, whichever Birchwood asshole unlocked my annex ruined the sweet, homey feeling I'd cherished. When I left, it was like a hurricane had swept through there. My poor bedspread—I cringed at the image of those three naked bodies writhing over my sheets.

No, I'd wait it out.

It takes the cool wash of dawn for the thumping bass to finally stop. Beads of dew cling to my ankles as I pick my way across the grass, weaving between empty beer bottles and abandoned suit jackets. Without the deep shadows to hide everyone's sins, the carnage of the grounds is bleak.

There are still a few stragglers: glamorous party-goers who are far less intimidating when passed out snoring in the shrubbery. I step over or around them, ignoring them all except for one guy who looks so peaky I stop to check his pulse. He groans and swats my hand away, and I take that as my cue to move on.

The practical thing to do would be to enter through the mansion and take stock of the damage. Then, after a power nap on literally any surface but my bed, I could attack the clean-up with some kind of plan.

I go straight to the annex back door. Screw practicality: I'm weepy from exhaustion, and if I bump into one of the Birchwood boys sprawled over the kitchen floor I can't guarantee I won't stomp on their neck. Pulling the skeleton key out from my sweatshirt, I breathe out a sigh when I find the door still locked.

"Home, sweet fucking home."

I toe my Docs off while I re-lock the door, and tug my sweatshirt over my head as I stumble to my bedroom door.

"Taken!" A voice calls when I rattle the doorknob.

What. The. Fuck. I slam my hand against the door, breathing hard, momentarily speechless with fury.

"Fuck off, will you?" Another voice yells.

I pinch the bridge of my nose and try to focus on slow breaths, just like when I had tantrums as a kid. I pull in a big lungful of air and let it out slowly, counting to ten, but when I'm done, I'm still so mad there are spots floating in my vision.

The door is locked from the inside; only Eli or one of the other Birchwood boys could have a key. If one of them has used my room to hook up, I will burn down this whole mansion, bet be damned.

"Get dressed, you intolerable ass wipes."

My key turns easily in the lock. The door swings open and I step inside, hands shaking with rage.

It's not just one Birchwood boy. It's all damn four of them.

Jasper sits with his back to my bed frame, a hickey staining his pale throat. His forearms drape over his knees and he stares at the ceiling, head tipped back. The fucker doesn't even spare me a glance, but Eli looks over from where he sits in my desk chair like a throne. Nate snores from beneath my bed covers, and Maddox sprawls on the floor—propped against the wall the same way he leaned against that tree in the grove.

They don't wear masks—just bare disdain and boredom on their faces.

Hurt pinches my chest. Clearly, it was the champagne, but I'd fooled myself into thinking Maddox had softened towards me. When our eyes snag, he pulls himself up to sit straighter, and his features are strained.

Good. Let him squirm.

"Out all night, Layla?" Eli sounds as fresh as a fucking daisy. "Well, you're nothing if not consistent."

I pour all the poison coursing through my veins into the words I spit back at him.

"Hiding from your own party, Eli? Why—ruined another girl's life?"

His face darkens, but it's Jasper that speaks.

"Give it a rest, both of you." He addresses the ceiling, eyes closed, like his head is too heavy to hold up. "My head is pounding. Can we please have a moment of bloody peace?"

"You will find it," I grind out, "in your *own room*. Get the hell out of mine." I round on Maddox and Eli, lip curled into a snarl. "All of you. Out."

I step forward to toss Nate's sleeping body from my bed, but Jasper's hand snaps up and wraps around my wrist. His grip is hard enough to bruise, and I wrench free, heart thudding.

For the first time, it hits home that I'm alone in a room with four guys who hate my guts. All four of them are bigger than me; all four have the money and family connections to make problems like me go away.

I snatch the broom from earlier and back up until my shoulders hit the wall.

"If you touch me, you'll regret it." I stare at Jasper, then Maddox, then Eli, holding their gaze so they can see I mean it. "I swear to God, if you hurt me I'll make your lives hell."

"Calm the fuck down, no one's going to hurt you." Jasper pushes to his feet, palms held up like he's trying to soothe a wild animal. "We're not monsters."

I snort and glance at a very pale Eli. "Could have fooled me."

Even so, my racing heartbeat slows. Their obvious horror at the very suggestion is far more reassuring than whatever Jasper might say.

I toss the broom to the floor. "You have thirty seconds to explain why you are in my room. If it's not a good reason, if it's just some stupid prank, I'll go to *your* rooms and burn your shit."

"It's Nate." Maddox's smoky voice is hoarse, like he's been talking non-stop for hours. When I look at him, he holds my gaze, eyes boring into mine. "He's... not well. We had to get him somewhere private."

Nate snuffles against my pillow, like he can hear us in his sleep. A tiny crack splinters through my outrage. I gather it up again, wrap it around myself like armor.

"Why not one of your rooms?"

"There were crowds everywhere—no way to sneak him through. This was the only option."

I cross my arms. "There's the pool house storage cupboard," I say, but my words have lost their force. The boys can sense it too, because their bodies relax an inch.

Great. An entire night without sleep, the beginnings of a hangover curdling my stomach, and no chance of rest. Not without kicking a sick person out of my bed, and I can't be that awful. Not even to Nate Becker.

I scrub my hands over my face and speak through my fingers. "Three people screwed on my bed last night."

Jasper barks out a laugh and tries to cover it with a cough. "We'll let Nate know."

"You can wash my sheets, too. And the bedspread."

His grin seems genuine. "Yes, ma'am."

Eli claps his hands together and rises from my desk chair. "Glad we're in agreement. We'll deal with your room, Layla, and you can hop to work and clean the rest of the house."

Just like that, the reluctant smile slides off my face. All those bottles and stains, all the carnage in every room—the thought rises up in a wave and threatens to drown me.

I turn without a word, stiff and numb, and dig through my closet for a fresh uniform.

"Let her sleep, man." Maddox stands and comes an arm's length from me. "Look at her: she's dead on her feet."

"You're the one who kept her up last night," Jasper mutters, and Eli's head whips around to stare at us both. I flush, grab my clothes and a towel, and get the hell out of that room.

Whatever Eli has to say, I know one thing: I don't want to hear it.

* * *

When I was a kid, I used to put all my homework off until there was a mountain of assignments looming over me. I'd get to Sunday evening and the sheer size of my mistake—the hours and hours ahead of me, spent craning over the kitchen table—rendered me frozen. Paralyzed.

More weekends than not, Mom found me like that, hyperventilating and cursing my terrible choices.

"Just take it one step at a time, sweetheart." She never got mad; she knew it upset me enough for both of us. I can hear the soothing lilt of her voice now. "Focus on baby steps and before you know it, they'll add up to a mile."

Even on the other side of the country, Mom makes everything better.

81

"Baby steps, baby steps," I mutter to myself as I work my way through the house. I don't let myself think about the next room or the one after that: the square meter I'm stood in is the only space that exists.

It helps that I need the distraction. Walking into my room this morning and finding all four boys in there threw me for a loop. And Jasper's chuckle, Maddox's honeyed voice sticking up for me, even the look on Eli's face when he heard Maddox and I spent time together...

I don't know what to make of it. I need to put my brain on standby mode and let my body take over for a while. Sure, I'd rather fire up the yoga app on my phone or wander round the gardens, but cleaning isn't so bad. Before long, I've worked up a decent sweat and strands of my hair stick to my forehead.

"You missed a bit."

Jasper leans in the doorway, hair damp and cheeks pink from the shower. I haven't seen him in this room before: it's some kind of fancy rec room, with squashy sofas strewn around a wall-mounted TV. There's a giant pool table on the Turkish rug, and a mahogany bar, complete with shelves of spirits and utterly wrecked by the party, lines the far wall.

I huff, stood in a halo of cleanliness in an otherwise trashed room. "I don't see it. Where exactly?"

Jasper's lips twitch, and he pushes away from the door frame. I swear, he is physically incapable of standing up straight when there is something to prop himself against: in almost every glimpse I've had of him, he's leaned against a wall or a cupboard or the fridge.

I expect some kind of snarky remark, but my mouth drops open as Jasper Wood begins to clean. He grabs a garbage bag from my pile of supplies and makes his way around the room, tossing empty bottles and plastic cups and God-knows-what-else inside.

I watch him for a moment, dumbstruck, then get back to work myself. If I try to make conversation he'll definitely leave, and no way am I going to scare off an extra pair of hands.

Through the open doorway, the sounds of the last few guests float up the stairs. Eli ushers them out, all businesslike charm, then the front door snaps shut and the house is quiet at last.

If it surprised me to see Jasper take up a garbage bag, I'm speechless when we move to the next room and find Maddox already cleaning. Yellow rubber gloves stretch up his forearms, the muscles flexing beneath as he scrubs at the sticky sheen on a tabletop.

"Hi," I choke out, and Maddox's lips curl in a slight smile. He keeps working, elbowing Jasper when he walks past, and I shake my head before grabbing my sponge.

If this is a prank, I don't care.

Baby steps, baby steps.

After a while, Eli finds the three of us cleaning the master bathroom. He watches us from the doorway, his intense eyes taking in Jasper bagging garbage while Maddox scrubs at the sink. His jaw clenches when he sees me knelt in the giant sunken bathtub, big enough to fit at least four people with steps leading down into it.

I look away, concentrating on the arc of my sponge on the tub bottom. The scum of dried bubbles lines the bathtub sides, and I try not to think about what my bare legs are kneeling on. When I risk a glance at Eli through my hair, the doorway is empty.

I guess not all the Birchwood boys want to help with cleaning up.

"Is Nate okay?" I finally ask in a guest bedroom, hours after we began. My arms ache from scrubbing and I'm dizzy from bleach fumes.

Jasper grumbles something under his breath, but Maddox answers me. "He'll sleep it off." He quirks a smile. "Thanks to you."

I nod, a blush creeping over my face, and ignore how Jasper rolls his eyes. Actually—screw that.

"You're wearing jeans, Jasper." He raises his eyebrow and I school my face to look innocent. "Has there been a death in the family?"

Silence rings through the room, then Maddox throws back his head and laughs.

"This is insubordination," Jasper says, but his eyes sparkle when he looks at me.

We finish the worst of the clean-up by mid-afternoon, and I ignore the siren song of the kitchen to stagger straight to bed. I'm so tired, my vision swims as I walk, and I bounce off the walls twice.

My bedroom door swings open, and I rub my eyes. It's spotless—cleaner than before the party, even—my bed made up with freshly laundered sheets and a wool blanket. My poor bedspread is nowhere to be seen, but it's probably for the best; my stomach is still wobbly from the champagne.

I lean back against the closed door and heave a sigh.

Home sweet home.

I collapse on my bed, shoes and all, and sink into sleep.

Chapter 8

"Okay, I'll admit it. You're a freaking genius. This summer is insane."

Pierce stretches her arms overhead, writhing on her towel. Her sunglasses perch daintily on her nose, and golden sand dusts her bare stomach and thighs. My best friend has always been solar-powered, curling up in patches of sunshine like a cat. This beach must be heaven for her, with its warm, soft sand and sparkling blue water.

Yup. I can finally say I've seen the sea. I've skipped like a crazy person into the waves, shrieking at the cold. I've built sandcastles and sunbathed and eaten ice cream that's gritty with sand.

Today is the perfect day.

I snap a photo to send to my parents, feeling a million miles away from the still, spicy heat of Santa Fe. Here, the wind snags at my hair and leaves salt crusting my skin.

I feel so freaking alive.

"I can't believe those assholes let you take a day off."

I flop onto my stomach, reaching back to untie my bikini strings. There will be no weird tan lines for this girl: I'm going all in.

"It's not like they had a choice. It's in our contract." I pillow my cheek on my forearms and watch Pierce squeeze sun tan lotion into her palm. "Besides, they haven't been as… dick-ish, lately."

Pierce scoffs, but I chew on my lip. It's true: since the house party two weeks ago, a kind of fragile peace has reigned. The boys don't snarl or hurl insults when I enter a room anymore, and in turn I've been doing my best impression of the quiet, dutiful maid. I clean up, help Diego prep the dinners, and most of all, I stay out of their way.

If this is all it takes to win that bet, that is a-okay with me.

Eli still tenses up when I'm near, and Nate snaps when he speaks to me, but he's like that with everyone. And even when he's vicious, I hold the truth to Nate Becker in my room. Three days after he kicked me out of my own bed, I walked in to find a parcel wrapped in brown paper and tied with string on my desk.

When I teased the paper open, I swear my heart dropped to my stomach. There, sitting on my desk, was a midnight blue bedspread—hand-stitched, and embroidered with the galaxy. Moons, stars, planets, bursting with color on the soft, dark material. And folded inside, a note tucked away with Nate's chicken scrawl.

'So next time I don't have to risk fucking herpes.'

I tucked the bedspread over my sheets and slid the note into the back of my journal.

"Don't waste another second of heartache on those jerks." Pierce frowns down at me, her lips pursed into what I privately think of as her schoolteacher face. "They made you so miserable, Layla, the last thing you need is to cozy up to them now. Have you forgotten how much they tortured you?"

I squeeze handfuls of my towel. "I'll never forget."

"Good." Pierce smiles and taps my hand—a peace offering. "I know surfing is on your summer bucket list. Let's find a hot guy to teach you."

I open my mouth to argue some more but a body drops to the sand between us. Our heads whip around and I can't stop the squeal of glee when I see Diego. He grins at us, messy brown curls waving in the breeze. He looks younger without his glasses, his brown eyes crinkled in amusement.

"What's this I hear about a bucket list? Perhaps I can be of service."

One look at my treacherous best friend tells me she's swooning. But how can I blame her? With the gorgeous brown skin of his chest on display and his lyrical accent, Diego has that effect.

Plus, he's a gentleman. Those seem to be rare around here.

"I have a list of things I want to do this summer. Adventures I want to have while I'm on the coast. Surfing lessons are on the list."

It sounds horribly childish when I say it out loud, but Diego hums and nods like I'm an intellectual. I bet he's a hit at dinner parties.

"I'll teach you, Layla Maid."

A few clusters of sunbathers over, Diego's friends are hollering. I brace for him to hop up and charge off with his usual manic energy, leaving his offer for another day, but I haven't given Diego enough credit. He waves back, gesturing for them to carry on without him, then smiles expectantly at the two of us.

Huh. I guess even with our truce, the Birchwood boys have primed me for rejection. Fuck, Pierce is right. We only have six more weeks of summer, and I won't let them ruin it like they did my second year. 'Not actively awful' will not be my benchmark for guys.

"Well, ladies?" Diego's grin is all white, shiny teeth. "Are you feeling brave?"

Hell yeah.

* * *

Diego walks me back to the mansion once we're too sore and battered to carry on, both of us caked in sand and wild-eyed. A constant grin splits my face, and I feel electric. Damn, I love surfing.

We part ways at a branching stone path, one way leading to the pool house and one to my annex. Diego scoops me off the ground into a crushing hug against his bare chest.

"I'll see you later, Layla Maid," he says as I kick my feet and laugh. "Call me if you get lost."

I watch his back as he walks away, skin warm in the sun, melting into a puddle. By the time I spin around and set off down the path, I'm practically dehydrated.

"You two look cozy."

Eli and Nate sprawl on a stone bench, dressed only in swim trunks. When I get close, I can smell the chlorine on their skin.

"We are." I shrug. I won't apologize about someone liking me here. "I guess Diego doesn't feel like toeing your party line."

I had friends on campus, back before these assholes turned on me. More friends than just Pierce, I mean. I smiled at people in the quad and they smiled back; I had study groups and coffee meet-ups.

Eli rolls his eyes, and I glare at the boy who took all that from me.

Nate cuts in before we can start sniping. "What's got you so riled up, Layla Maid?"

He nods at my sand-caked skin, my windswept hair tangled with salt, my bright eyes. And maybe that bedspread has turned me soft, but I beam at the grumpy ass.

"Surfing. Or falling in, anyway. Turns out I can't balance for shit."

He chuckles at the glee in my voice, eyes flicking back down over my body. I tossed on a pair of shorts before we left the beach, but my top half is bare except for my bikini. His gaze scorches a trail over my skin, and I shiver even in the heat.

"Put your tongue back in, Becker." Eli stays sprawled, like he's loose and relaxed, but the tension is clear in every line of his body. "The last thing we need is you panting after the help."

Nate doesn't even look at him. Everyone—me included—always thinks of Eli as the leader of the Birchwood boys. He's always the one setting the tone and making the plans. But at crunch time, I'm not so sure he has them leashed.

"Are you going to the bonfire tonight?"

Nate's voice is low. Like the two of us are alone somewhere dark and secret, not out in the afternoon sun with Eli bitching beside us. Eli curses and pushes to his feet, striding down the path towards the house.

Nate doesn't spare him a glance.

"Yeah—yes." I stammer when I find my voice. The tattoo inked over Nate's chest is seriously distracting. It swirls in intricate patterns, hinting at shadows and shapes, and I wish I could inspect it properly. "It's still my day off." Defensiveness bleeds into my tone. "Diego invited me."

Nate smirks and pushes to his feet, suddenly close enough

to touch. A bead of moisture slides down his chest. I lick my lips.

He leans in close, like he's telling me a secret, and his breath tickles my neck. "Let's hope the chef will share."

He turns and follows Eli back to the path, and I gape at his back.

Holy shit.

* * *

The flames crackle and leap at the stars, as tall as any man on the beach. The orange glow from the bonfire casts harsh shadows on faces and paints everyone with the same buttery warmth. All around, half-dressed bodies are grinding to the music, bare skin sliding over each other, or clustered in groups, swigging from bottles and laughing.

Pierce pinches my elbow. "Hell is empty," she murmurs, lips curling up.

"And the devils are here."

The warmth of the fire washes over us as we approach, and I hum as the heat licks my skin. Savage joy courses through me, making me light-headed. It's the stars, the flames, the pulsing music; the groping, grinding bodies. Pierce and I already passed a bottle of vodka back and forth on the walk over, and the buzz makes my eyes shine and my hips swing as we walk.

"Layla!"

Diego waves at me, stumbling away from the press of bodies. Pierce nudges me and slinks away, promising to find drinks.

We meet in the halo of light from the bonfire, and I realize with a jolt that Diego is dragging a man by the hand.

"This is Alejandro." Diego tugs the man to stand next to him, and I take in his floppy black hair and chiseled jaw. The two of them together are like a centerfold in a magazine. I nod and offer a smile.

So much for my little crush.

"Have you seen those boys are here?" Diego's eyes are concerned, protective. He always calls them 'those boys', refusing to remember their names on principle ever since I told him what they did to me on campus.

I didn't even tell him the worst things, either. I don't know why I'm protecting them.

The memory of Maddox's thighs braced under mine, the scorching trail of Nate's eyes over my skin—they flick through my mind. Why am I burning up for a group of guys who hate my guts? I must be freaking damaged.

"We'll keep them away from you." Diego nods at Alejandro, mistaking my twitchy guilt for fear.

I blurt out before I think better of it. "No, don't do that. I can torture them better up close."

Diego throws his head back and laughs, and Alejandro gives me a confused smile.

"Revenge. Yes, Layla Maid. I like it." Diego takes my hand, winking at his date as he pulls us both onto the makeshift dance floor. "And I know just where to start."

We squeeze through the press of bodies until we're stood with me sandwiched between the two men. Over Diego's shoulder, I spot all four Birchwood boys drinking and laughing together. A few girls are there too, tossing their hair and draping themselves over the boys' shoulders, and vicious jealousy tears through me at the sight.

Diego reaches around my waist, tugging Alejandro close

until he's pressed along my back. Then, in front of everyone, the gorgeous chef slides a leg between my thighs.

Holy crap.

With Diego's lead, the three of us sway, finding the beat. I'm so frazzled by the hot men lined up against me that I keep bumping into them, losing time, but Diego grips my hips and takes charge. After a minute, I fall into the rhythm. The buzz from the vodka loosens my tensed muscles, and Diego slides his hands up my waist, leaving my hips to shake and sway. Alejandro takes his place, hands gripping the waistband of my shorts, and I tip my head back against this hot stranger's shoulder and close my eyes.

I forget the girls touching the Birchwood boys, forget our little scheme, lost in the music and movement.

Angry cursing breaks the spell, bringing me back to earth. I lift my head and stare into the flushed face of Eli Henderson. He glares at the three of us, at the fluid way our hips move together, the way I'm crowded between them.

I hold his gaze and roll my body against Diego.

Eli snatches the drink out of Jasper's hand and storms off through the crowd. The girl he was just talking to blinks after him, her hand still raised.

"Is it working, Layla Maid?" Diego murmurs in my ear, sweat damp against his temple. "Are those boys sick with wanting you?"

I look at the three remaining boys, at the tight grip of their hands on their bottles and the way their eyes fix on our every move. I nod, and Diego leans over my shoulder to capture Alejandro's mouth in a biting kiss.

Jasper's eyebrows shoot up his forehead.

Nate grins at me and I grin back.

"Jesus Christ, I leave you alone for five minutes and you're starring in a porno."

Pierce's words are harsh, but amusement dances in her eyes. We break apart and she hands me a drink, tugging me away from the thick crowd of dancers. Diego and Alejandro stay put, so wrapped up in each other now that they barely notice me leaving.

We've only just found a spot before Nate is there, slinging an arm around my shoulder. Jasper steps up to my other side and I glance around for Maddox, but he's long gone.

"Who knew our grumpy little maid could move like that?" Nate breathes in my ear. Pierce shoots him a glare to shrivel balls.

"Fuck off, Becker. It's her day off. Your stupid bet can wait."

"Who said anything about the bet?" Nate's finger traces a line up my arm and I fight a full body shiver. Jasper watches his friend's hand with detached interest. "Maybe I just want to see those moves up close."

He grabs my hand and I let him. Now it's my turn to face Pierce's scorn.

She rounds on me, eyes wide in disbelief.

"You cannot be fucking serious."

"It's just a dance." I shrug weakly, hand clasped in Nate's. "What's the big deal?"

Pierce breathes out hard, nostrils flaring. She flicks her eyes to Nate and Jasper, then fixes them back on me.

"Don't cry to me when they mess you up this time. I don't want to fucking hear it."

I nod, voice trapped in my throat, then my best friend leaves. She shoves her way through the crowd, shoulders around her ears.

Fuck. I go to follow her, but Nate pulls me back.

I wrench my hand away, but it's Jasper that speaks. "You've gone to all this trouble. Might as well see if it was worth it."

His eyes are bright, roaming over my face and body, and when his tongue flicks over his bottom lip, heat flares in my core. I glance at Nate, but he's no better: his pupils are dilated, his hands shoved deep in his pockets like he'll grab for me otherwise.

"Just one dance."

My voice is hoarse, and triumph sharpens their features. Jasper holds up his hand like we're at a freaking regency ball, then pulls me deep into the crush of bodies.

* * *

Jasper Wood is the last person on Earth I'd have predicted to be a good dancer. He's always so stiff and straight-laced, buttoned into crisp shirts and silk waistcoats.

He's not buttoned up tonight. He's in gray jeans and a black t-shirt, the cotton sliding over his chest.

And he's not just a good dancer. He's *fucking incredible.*

The music pulses with a Latino swing, and Jasper takes my hand and pulls me close. His fingers slide around my rib cage, his leg slots between mine, and then we're rocking together. Heat blazes over every inch of me that touches him, shorting out my brain like a power surge.

There's no way he doesn't feel me shudder and press closer.

His grip tightens on my waist.

I've lost my damn mind, but I don't care. Not with Jasper's blue eyes holding mine. Not with his plump mouth quirking up at the corners. I sweep my hair back and hold it there, rolling my body against him.

His groan vibrates through me. I feel it to my damn toes, bare and curling in the sand.

The music changes; slows and darkens. It's taut and teasing: a beat to grind to. To fuck to.

I smirk up at Jasper through my lashes, but a second body presses up behind me. My lips open on a sigh; I hold Jasper's eyes while Nate grips my hip with one hand and bands an arm around my stomach. Jasper's lips part as he stares down at the muscled arm pulling me flush against his friend.

His eyes flick up to mine and my stomach swoops. His pupils are so dilated his blue eyes are nearly black, and I'm burning up here pressed between two guys I hate.

He loves this. He's so fucking into it.

He's not the only one.

"You didn't think I'd let him have all the fun, did you?"

Nate's teeth scrape my earlobe; my legs turn to jelly. Only his arm wrapped around my waist holds me up, the muscles hard and defined, and I run my palm over the tattooed skin. He chuckles darkly into my hair.

The crowd shifts around us, and I glimpse Pierce. She's dancing with a guy, smiling up at him and flicking her hair, but her eyes dart over to us and her smile falters. Guilt washes through me, sickly and cold, dousing the inferno Nate and Jasper have set burning in my core. They must feel me stumble, because they steer me around effortlessly until Pierce is out of sight.

"Get out of your head, Layla Maid."

It's Jasper this time, nipping at my ear. A bottle of vodka thrusts over my shoulder and Jasper takes it, swigging deep. The column of his throat is pale, flushed pink where it meets his chest, and I lick a stripe up the hollow. He splutters the vodka, spilling a few drops onto the sand before he offers it to me.

I grip it and swig. It's a terrible decision waiting to happen, along with a God-awful hangover, but I push those thoughts from my head. I didn't come here to overthink and fret. I'm here to feel alive.

And hell, do I feel alive. With two sculpted, warm bodies at my front and back, two guys glued to every swing of my hips, I'm electric. Powerful.

I swallow another mouthful of vodka, and I swear I could level towns.

The body at my back moves away, cold air rushing in, and I go to turn around and drag Nate back, but a hard chest crowds against me again.

I hum, tipping my head back onto Nate's shoulder. Jasper watches me, eyes hungry and smirk spreading wider, and I reach for Nate's arm to slide back around my waist. His hand spreads out on my rib cage, thumb grazing my breast.

"Feeling bold, Becker?"

I grin and glance back, only to find Eli staring down at me. My mouth drops.

Even wrapped around me until his heat scorches my back, even grinding against my ass to the music, he looks fucking haughty.

It pisses me off—what, he thinks he's so much better than me in this moment? I roll my ass back against Eli's crotch, smirking in triumph when he frowns and tightens his grip on my hip. His thumb grazes my breast again, more deliberate this time, and Jasper runs his thumb over my jaw.

I'm catching fire. My head swims—from the drink, yes, but

mostly from Jasper and Eli. I'm drunk on the way they grip and stroke me, like they can't take their hands away. Like I'm theirs. Jasper runs his palms *everywhere*, anywhere on my body that's not straight up public indecency.

He touches me like he's planning ahead. Like he's mapping the land for a future invasion.

Eli's grip is firm; just this side of bruising. Frustration bleeds through his pores and roughens his movements until he's leading all three of us from behind.

He hates that he wants me.

Me? I'm giddy with it.

The music changes again, a bluesy vibe with a thrumming beat, and Eli stiffens behind me like he's waking from a dream. He ducks his head and his breath is cool on my sweat-damp skin.

"Ever the tease, Layla. Some things never change."

It's a bucket of icy water. I place my palms against Jasper's chest and shove.

He stumbles back, hands up and face confused, but I don't speak to either of them. I elbow my way free of the knot of people and take off across the sand.

Dozens of judging eyes rake over my skin, but when I glare back, they turn away.

Pierce doesn't even notice—too wrapped up in her new guy, arms draped around his neck.

Tears burn my eyes, but I force a smile and wave when I pass Diego and Alejandro. They sit cuddled up near the bonfire, arms tangled, and their easy intimacy steals the oxygen from my lungs.

I can't remember the last time someone touched me like that. Not with heat, but with tenderness.

It's the vodka doing this. Making me maudlin. But I knew what I was doing when I took this fucking bet.

I knew who I was dancing with when I let them hold me. When I rolled my hips against them and touched them back.

My legs are numb as I stumble along the beach. I raise my damp eyes, and the stars slide into lines.

* * *

I barely have time to down a glass of water before there's a soft knock at the annex door. There are maybe five people that could be: Diego, or one of the Birchwood boys. Pierce is wrapped around some guy at the bonfire, thinking she told me so.

I chew my lip and drum my fingers on the kitchen counter. The annex kitchen is nothing like the main house: in here, it's all plastic counter tops and cheap linoleum. The knock comes again, soft and hesitant, and a dark shape shifts behind the frosted glass of the kitchen door.

Tall and broad shouldered. That could be any of them, really, though the shape is too still for Diego.

I count to three, set my shoulders, and wrench the door open. Maddox leans in and places his palm flat on the door, like I might slam it in his face.

"I saw you leave the beach. You seemed upset."

God. Is it not enough for these boys to bat me around between them like a toy? Do they have to rub it in, too?

"I left because I want to be alone."

Maddox steps inside and leans his forearm against the door. His hair hangs around my face like a curtain, and I smell the wood smoke clinging to him from the bonfire.

"What did Eli say to you?"

I snort. "Nothing the rest of you haven't said a thousand times."

Maddox doesn't like that, his mouth tightening, but I'm done with this conversation. If he won't take the hint and leave willingly, I'll bore him out the door.

Turning back to my kitchen, I fill the battered old kettle I fished out of a cupboard in my first week. I take my favorite mug out of the cupboards, the one with pandas on it, then pause, staring at the row of cups.

My mom's face swims before me, her cheeks rosy and her kind eyes wrinkled.

I bow my head. "God damn it."

I fish a second mug out and place it on the countertop.

"You're too kind, Layla Maid."

Maddox steps fully into the kitchen, closing the door to the cool breeze blowing in from the garden. I'd forgotten how tiny the space is, but now we're filling it together: he leans against the fridge and I glue myself to the opposite counter.

"Do you have to call me that?"

His chuckle is quiet, smoky. "It's affectionate, I promise. What would you rather I call you?"

A whole list of traitorous options scroll through my mind, but I scoff and slam the cutlery drawer shut.

"How about my name?" I snap, stirring milk into our coffees so viciously that scalding liquid sloshes over the rims. Maddox takes it with milk, no sugar, like me. I hate that I know that.

"All right. *Layla.*"

His voice is wicked. Full of promise. I slam the spoon down on the counter and pass his mug without looking at him. When I finally muster the courage to look up, he blows gently on his coffee and watches me.

Maddox isn't like the other Birchwood boys. They're all jostling to be in the action, to draw admirers and awed respect. Maddox hangs back, but it's not because he's nervous.

He's a panther watching in the shadows.

"Did you like your dances?"

I take a hurried gulp of coffee and burn the inside of my mouth. Maddox smirks, steam curling past his lips, and raises an eyebrow, waiting me out.

"Yes."

There's no point lying: he saw me out there on the sand. He saw the eager way his friends gripped me; the way I touched them back.

Maddox nods, almost to himself. I'm starting to think he never asks a question he doesn't already know the answer to. It's like a test, but I can't bring myself to be annoyed. Instead, I watch him, heart skittering in my chest, suddenly eager to see how he reacts.

"Did you like dancing with all three? Did you like being passed between them?"

I bristle at the innuendo, but Maddox is serious. His eyes dart over my face, cataloging my features like he can read my thoughts in my bitten lips, my tired eyes.

"Yes," I say, and this time I hurl the truth at him like a weapon. I loved being dwarfed by two hard chests; I loved being stroked by three sets of hands. Even now, after Eli tossed it all in my face, I'm still wet and aching in my core.

Maddox takes a sip of his coffee, hums, then sets the mug down.

"I liked it too."

His mouth on mine is sudden and hungry. One hand tugs

my mug out of my grip, then his fingers plunge into my hair. He tilts my head back to find the perfect angle, thrusting his tongue against mine.

I groan, clutching handfuls of his t-shirt. The way his tongue slides in and out, stroking me: he's fucking my mouth. It's all I can do to hold on, raising up on my tiptoes to give as good as I get. Our hips seal together, grinding like we're dancing to our own music now, and I burn everywhere he touches me.

Finally we break apart, gasping for breath. Maddox rests his forehead against mine, chest heaving, and I can taste his coffee on my tongue.

He runs the pad of one thumb along my collarbone, slipping beneath the strap of my tank top. The scrape of his calluses tickles my skin, and my nipples harden in my bra.

Maddox takes his thumb away, squeezing at my hip instead.

"Back to work, tomorrow."

I nod. I lost the ability to form sentences several minutes ago.

Maddox smiles, dark and curling, but I'm not afraid. Not even when he places his mouth against my temple and murmurs, pressing the words directly into my skin.

"I look forward to it."

Something tells me this isn't a threat. That it's not about the bet.

And so, for the first time, I look forward to it too.

Chapter 9

Eli Henderson is and will always be a dick. At 9am—an ungodly hour for the amount of vodka I drank last night—he calls me out onto the driveway. I obey his summons, grumbling and squinting against the bright sunshine, already baking everything it touches. It's going to be another long shift of flushed, itchy skin and my thick maid's dress sticking to my damp back.

Eli, of course, is cool and unruffled. He looks like he's been up for hours, showered and clad in a pressed blue shirt. He stands with his hands clasped behind his back, politely waiting for me to drag my hungover corpse closer.

"Make her shine," he says, unbearably smug, and raps on the roof of his Bentley. The constant breeze that rolls in off the ocean tousles his dark hair.

"Do fuck off, Eli."

I know I'm pushing my luck, and I brace as his eye twitches in annoyance. But then his face smooths back into that polite, blank mask.

"Remind me why you're here, Layla?"

Ugh. "I'm your feckless, slutty maid."

Even Eli can't hide the dimple that flashes in his cheek. I'd probably find it adorable, if I could focus on anything beyond my pounding headache and dry mouth. "Don't forget 'perennially hungover.'"

My gut roils. "If only I could."

This has been a shockingly lighthearted conversation considering the asshole I'm having it with. It's almost a relief, comfortingly familiar, when he tosses a sponge at me. My reflexes are still pickling in half a liter of cheap vodka, and it bounces off my chest and lands at my feet.

"Thank God." I pluck at the damp imprint of the sponge on my dress and wrinkle my nose at the smell. "You were nearly friendly for a minute there, Eli."

It's like I've flipped a switch. His spine straightens; his eyes narrow. He steps closer, and for a split second I think he's going to push me against the Bentley. I lick my lips, shifting my weight, but he keeps himself on a tight leash.

"Just do your damn job. Clean the house, wash my car, and keep out of everyone's way." He reaches to straighten a tie he's not wearing, then huffs and stalks back down the driveway.

"Easiest forty grand I ever made!" I yell at his back. My gut swoops and I shut the hell up, one hand on my rampaging stomach.

Breathe in. Breathe out. Don't vomit on the rich boy's car.

By the time I quell the nausea and make the trip to fill two buckets with soap and water, there are two more assholes hanging around the Bentley.

"This is not my day," I say, more to myself than anyone else, as I heave the buckets down with a slosh. "Give me that."

Nate grins and launches the sponge like a baseball, blessing me with a second damp spot on my abdomen. Jasper roars with laughter, and I step around the pair of idiots with as much dignity as I can muster. Dunking the sponge in the soap bucket,

I drip a trail over Jasper's brogues before slapping it on the roof of the car.

"You know he's just doing this to torture you, right?"

Nate digs his teeth into his bottom lip, clearly thrilled about my predicament. Today he's in a tight white tank and khaki sweatpants, his olive skin bright and healthy. I glance at Jasper and scowl: no hangovers here, apparently.

"The soap will leave streaks," Jasper puts in. His tan chinos hug his thighs, while his long-sleeved black shirt sets off the gold in his hair. "Eli will get it professionally done as soon as you're finished sweating over it."

"Good," I grunt, my hair already sticking to my forehead. I try not to inhale too deeply; I *know* the alcohol is seeping out of my pores. "I won't try very hard, then."

I expect them to drift away and do whatever they do on these scorching summer days—go for a smug, non-hungover run, maybe—but they stay, flicking suds at each other and bickering. I have to barge them out the way so I can clean where they've planted their lazy asses.

"Don't you have places to be?" I snap, glaring down at the stupid car. "Lives to ruin? Unsuspecting women to seduce?"

Jasper whistles, long and low, and jerks his head towards the house. Nate jogs away, and a pang of regret shudders through my chest. I push it away. I can't deal with their bullshit not with vodka poisoning my insides. Not even after last night.

"Don't be that way, Layla Maid." Jasper's voice is soft and coaxing, and a different kind of shiver runs through me. "We've come to throw ourselves at your feet."

I snort and scrub harder. It's patently ridiculous. This is another Birchwood boy scheme, one cooked up and timed for when I'm at my most vulnerable.

They need to break me to win the bet. I haven't forgotten.

"Don't fucking bother, man." Nate's voice echoes down the driveway. "Get this down her first."

A tattooed arm thrusts over the Bentley, a steaming mug of coffee held out to me handle-first. I moan—an obscene, urgent sound—and snatch the mug from Nate's grip.

He watches me cradle it, inhaling the steam between sips, with dark satisfaction written on every inch of his face.

"Better?" Jasper watches my mouth, wetting his own lip when I dart my tongue out for a stray drop.

I moan again in reply.

Nate snorts. "Fuck, Mackenzie. If I knew all it took was a coffee to get noises like that, I'd have been bringing you breakfast in bed from day one."

I flush at the image of Nate with a breakfast tray, climbing onto my lumpy twin bed.

My back hits the Bentley as Nate and Jasper flank me on either side, eyes hungry as they watch me drink my coffee like it's a porno.

Jasper skates a finger down my neck, and hell—maybe it's about to become one.

That's how we're stood when Maddox rounds the corner. Both boys are crowding close, with Jasper stroking my neck while Nate nibbles my shoulder.

Guilt flares through me, hot and sickly, but the surprise on Maddox's face melts into a smirk. He shoves his hands into his jean pockets and props one shoulder against the brick mansion wall, apparently happy to watch his friends at work.

I stare at him, flustered and aching, as his words from last night echo through my mind.

"I liked it too."

105

His eyes follow Jasper's hands as they trace my rib cage and squeeze my hip, then flick to the trail Nate is blazing across my collarbone.

Finally, after what feels like an age, Maddox looks back up and meets my gaze head on. It's like someone jammed my finger in a plug socket: energy flows through me, from the soles of my feet to the tips of my fingers.

When I groan, it's loud enough for him to hear.

The rumble of an approaching car sends us flying apart, the boys cursing and adjusting their pants. I snatch up the sponge and scrub randomly at the car, like I can wash away the excitement staining my cheeks.

A car door slams, and heels pick their way up the driveway. I turn around, a bland smile plastered on my face, then falter when I see Georgia frowning down at me.

"Miss Mackenzie." She nods politely at the boys, and even though it's technically their house, they obey her clear dismissal. I watch Nate's back as he slouches away, my empty mug swinging in his hand.

"I won't dance around why I'm here. The agency has received a complaint."

"I—what?"

My first thought is Eli, but he'd been relatively cheery this morning. He'd practically joked around. The other three, I'm pretty sure they want me here—maybe to mess with me, but the end result is the same.

This doesn't make sense.

"An allegation has been made against you. Of… inappropriate relations with your guests."

Georgia frowns at the boys' retreating backs, then at the damp dress clinging to my chest and stomach, before pinning

106

me with a knowing glare.

Shame floods through me, with anger quick on its heels.

Fuck his cheery mood this morning. This has Eli written all over it.

* * *

I've always hated being in trouble. As a kid, when I got into scraps in school, just the sight of my teacher's irritated face used to give me a stomach ache. One time, when I bounced our ball into the neighbor's yard for the third time in ten minutes, I ran upstairs and hid under my bed rather than face all those frowns.

It drove Mom mad. *"You can't skulk your way out of this, young lady. Have some backbone and face up to what you've done."*

Honestly, it's a miracle I can stand to be around the Birchwood boys at all. Knowing they hate me, or hell—even mildly dislike me—makes me itchy all over.

This is turning out to be a very itchy summer. First the Birchwood boys, then Pierce, and now Georgia, the agency lady. All of them annoyed at me for one thing or another.

Seems like whatever I do to mend one bridge, another immediately collapses.

My bridge with Eli is down to one rotting, wobbly plank.

"What did the agency woman want?" Jasper calls as I march through the reception room. He's lounging sideways on an armchair, legs kicked up and ankles crossed. A hardback book rests in his lap, and a pair of glasses perch in his hair.

Mouth clamped shut, I round his chair and head for the staircase. I don't trust myself to speak. If I open my mouth, I may never close it again on the flood of bitterness building in my chest.

"Layla?"

My shoes smack against the marble steps. My fingernails dig into my palms, hard enough to leave red crescent marks, and I set my shoulders as I reach the top step.

Enough snide comments and sabotage. Eli Henderson will look me in the eye and explain who the fuck he thinks he is. And then, I will set the record straight about who, exactly, *I* am.

I won't roll over and take it. Not anymore. Fuck the bet.

The door to Eli's suite bangs open, and I sweep inside without knocking. Eli jerks up from where he sits on the bed, head cradled in his hands.

"What the fuck? Get out!"

My voice is deadly calm. "You nearly got me fired."

"What are you—"

"I'm on a final warning. What happened to our bet? What, you can't win fair and square so you'll just get rid of me?"

"I have no idea what you're talking about."

His panic at me barging in has faded from his eyes, leaving only cool disdain.

"I knew you'd be a sore loser, Eli, but I thought you'd at least have the self-respect to follow through. But then, that's not your strong suit, is it? Owning your decisions."

His eyes flash. Eli hates any mention of what happened between us, of how things ended—at least, any mention that's not on *his* terms.

But you know what? I'm done tip-toeing around Eli Henderson.

All the snide looks and whispers on campus; getting thrown out of campus parties. The email I got the day before my internship was due to start, with cold, formal lines about *'Ethical conduct'* and *'Protecting the gallery's reputation.'* It all scrolls through my mind like a slideshow, and I ball my hands into fists.

"You're pathetic, Eli Henderson. You tried to ruin my life at college over some imagined insult, and you're screwing me over again now."

Two spots of color glow high on his cheeks as I rant. See, he can claim not to care until his teeth fall out, but the loathing is clear in his tight shoulders, his trembling hands. When he speaks, the words rip out of him in a snarl.

"*Imagined* insult? Don't paint yourself as some innocent victim, Layla. Everything that's happened to you, you brought on yourself and more."

The laughter that peals out of me is mocking, cruel.

"You're right about that. I'm *so sorry*, Eli. I'm sorry I kissed you. I'm sorry I had a crush. I'm sorry for drinking that night, like literally every other person at the party. I'm even sorry we got caught."

I step closer as I talk, tugged towards him on invisible strings.

"But more than anything, I'm sorry that I ever came within fifty feet of you. If I'd known you were so fucking repressed, that you'd punish me like this, I'd have tried my luck with one of your friends instead."

His hands twitch, like he wants to throttle me right here. I'm close enough now that he could.

"Oh, I bet you would, Layla. That's what you're doing now, isn't it? Trying to fuck my friends to get back at me."

I give him a nasty smile. "Not everything is about you, Eli. Maybe I just want them."

I turn to go, marching towards the door, but I can't help but spin around and keep talking. These words have lodged like splinters in my chest for over a year. I've fantasized about this moment, about confronting Eli with what he did.

"I didn't force you to kiss me. Or to do more than that, either. You made your own damn choices, Eli. And it's not my fucking fault that some drunk dicks took photos. You think I *wanted* soft porn of myself all over the internet? You think I wanted my parents, my friends, to see that?"

My voice cracks, and I swallow hard. All the anger and hurt from the last year, all those ugly feelings that I pushed down and told myself I could pretend away, they're bubbling back up and spewing from me like a festering black cloud. And Eli's meeting me, blow for blow, his own stained soul on full display.

"Do you honestly expect me to believe that? You ruined my fucking career, Layla. You weren't the first to try that, either. I bet the media—hell, I bet my father's opponents lined your pockets for life."

I advance on him again, dragging in shuddering breaths.

"You're a smart guy, Eli." I jab my finger into his chest, hard. "If that's true, why am I wasting my summer washing your goddamn car? Why did I take this fucking bet?"

He snorts, slaps my hand away. "You've always been desperate."

But his words have lost their bite. Uncertainty flickers across his face, gone too fast to settle, and then his blank mask smooths over his features.

Maybe I finally made it through to Eli Henderson. And maybe I don't fucking care.

"Go to hell." I grit the words through my teeth. "Play fair, or I'll show you a real scandal. You think a couple of nudes are the worst that can happen to you? I'll show your precious daddy and the whole goddamn world what a wretch you really are."

I spin around and march out the door, slamming it over his reply.

* * *

Rage-cleaning truly is good for the soul. But with Eli on my case, there aren't enough spills and dust bunnies in the world to calm me down. By the end of the day, my arms are stiff and aching from angry scrubbing. By the end of the week, everyone is avoiding me and the mansion sparkles like never before.

It's not enough. I want to bite Eli's damn head off. I want to hogtie him and throw him in the pool.

"You know what I'm going to say."

Pierce kicks at a lump of driftwood, scraping it through the damp sand. At our side, the breakers dash themselves against the beach.

"Save your breath, then." I'm churlish tonight, lashing out at everyone and everything. Pierce takes it all in stride; she's seen me hurt by the Birchwood boys plenty of times before. She's a saint, honestly, for agreeing to meet me at all. But she didn't even hesitate: she picked up the phone, heard my choked plea, and changed back out of her pajamas.

I don't tell her it's so much worse this time. That when Maddox kissed me against that kitchen counter, when Jasper and Nate pressed me against the Bentley, I honestly believed something was brewing between us all.

Even with Eli.

111

How much of an idiot can I be?

"No, I need to say this. For my own satisfaction."

I groan, digging my elbow into her ribs. She dances away, a shadow in the dark. No stars tonight. No moonlight. Just heavy black clouds and spots of cold rain.

"Layla!" the shadow calls, glee in her husky voice. "I fucking told you so!"

I scoop a fistful of damp sand and chuck it in her direction, and Pierce cackles and takes off. I chase her until my legs shake and my throat is raw from sucking in cold, salty air. When I finally tackle her, we go down hard; the breath knocked out of us.

"Get off, you massive lump." Pierce wriggles out from under me and flops onto her back. I roll over and stare up at the same clouds, the same velvet dark. Spots of rain fleck my hot cheeks, but I don't brush them away.

"Why are you still there, Layla?"

Her voice is cautious. Careful. I screw my eyes shut, my throat suddenly tight.

"I don't know," I whisper eventually. "I know they probably won't even pay out. But it's like, when they're around, the life I could have had is right there. Dangling just out of reach. Having friends in college, going to parties and mixers, being happy and carefree."

I swallow hard. "Making my parents proud. Even... Eli. Having Eli. It's addictive. Even when it hurts, I go back for more."

Pierce sighs and rolls onto her side, her head pillowed on one arm. I can just make out her eyes in the darkness, the shadow of her mouth, her tangle of black hair.

"You danced with the others at the bonfire." Pierce ignores

my clear masochism, and I don't blame her. My baggage wouldn't fit in a moving truck, and she is only one girl. "Not just Eli. Are you sure it's him you want?"

I blow out a slow breath. In the dark, the breeze brushing cool over my skin, I can conjure the feel of Maddox's body. My palms remember the exact curve of his hip bones; my mouth dries at the memory of his tongue stroking mine. My heart thunders in my rib cage like he's really here, his body lowering over mine, pressing me into the sand.

"I kissed Maddox." Pierce sucks in a surprised breath. "Or really, he kissed me. In my kitchen, after the bonfire."

"Do you like him?"

"Yes." I steel myself for what I need to admit. My best friend has always had an open mind; with a colorful dating history of her own, she's not the type to judge.

This might prove too much, though, even for her.

"Pierce? I want them all. I know they're assholes, all four of them, and I know they hate me. I want them anyway."

For a long stretch of time, there's only the crash of waves and my thumping heart. Bile churns in my stomach.

Through all the worst moments of the last year, all of those days, weeks, and months at rock bottom—I had Pierce. She picked me up and dusted me off more times than I can count. I cannot lose her.

"Well, fuck," she says at last. "Who knew you were so ambitious?"

Relief flows through me, hot and sweet, and I snicker. "It's good to have a goal."

"Those poor boys." She's laughing now, too, and it's the best sound. "You almost have to feel sorry for them."

I scoff, pushing upright. "Don't. It's never going to happen.

113

I'll finish this summer with what's left of my dignity and leave here forty grand richer. And in the meantime, I'll find enough dirt on the four of them that they'll have to leave me alone at college."

Pierce whistles. "Espionage. I love it." We scramble to our feet and head back the way we came, damp clothes chafing as we walk. "Don't get caught," she adds after a minute. "The agency will hang you out to dry."

I huff, fingers twitching at my sides.

"Don't I know it."

Neither of us states the obvious. If the Birchwood boys catch me snooping, I'll be begging the agency to send me home.

* * *

Jasper never locks his bedroom door. He leaves it propped open, the orderly rows of books and neat stacks of folded clothes visible from the hallway. Up to now, I've marched past with my eyes averted, determined that Jasper will never accuse me of stalking him the way Eli does.

Today, I linger. Duster in hand, I step up to the doorway, the toes of my black sneakers touching the exact border between hallway and bedroom.

He's not home. None of them are. They loaded into Nate's blood-red sports car and peeled down the driveway an hour ago. They'll be gone for hours, doing whatever it is they do when they're away from the mansion. Terrorizing the local towns, probably.

That leaves plenty of time for me to 'clean'. I clench the duster in my damp palm and step into Jasper's bedroom.

It smells like him. Like fresh air and clean linens. The bed

114

is made, the cream covers pulled tight enough to bounce a quarter off, and the window above the desk hangs open. A breeze flows through the room, ruffling a stack of papers on the desk.

I slide a drawer open, ignoring the pinch of guilt. Last week, Jasper traced his finger up my neck and gazed down at me with something like wonder in his eyes. Since then, I've avoided all of them like they're diseased, ducking out of rooms when they enter and feigning deafness when they call my name.

It's all about the bet. I have to remember. Because for a stupid moment there, the desire in his eyes, in his touch—it felt real.

A leather-bound notebook and a fountain pen rest inside the drawer. I've seen Jasper writing in this book, curled up at the base of a tree or draped over a stone bench in the gardens. He flips it closed and smiles when someone walks past, thumb holding the cover down.

If there *is* something I can hold over him, some kind of insurance against further torment… it's in that book.

I stare down at worn gray cover and well-thumbed pages, heart thumping and blood roaring in my ears. *This is what you came for,* I urge myself, but my arms glue to my sides. *Don't go soft on them now—*

I slam the drawer shut. The desk rocks from the impact, the stack of papers sliding into disarray, and I neaten them with trembling fingers. A flash of the duster over the surface of the wood, and I'm out the door, feet pounding down the hallway.

For God's sake. What is it about these assholes that burrows under my skin?

I don't bother trying Maddox's or Nate's rooms. With them, too, the earth has shifted under my feet and, bet or no bet, I'm no longer sure where I stand. But if there's a chance of a real truce—one not forced by blackmail—I want to take it.

Eli is another matter.

His bedroom door is locked, naturally. I wouldn't expect any less of the paranoid jerk. Except maybe he's not so paranoid after all, since my skeleton key slides easily into the lock. The door opens with a click, swinging open to the master bedroom.

I didn't look around last time I was here. I was too busy yelling, vision tunneled by rage. It's more tasteful than I expected: Turkish rugs on polished oak floorboards, bookcases crammed with everything from leather hardbacks to magazines. The oil paintings on the walls are originals, the peaks and swirls of paint depicting the coast, the local town, these gardens.

Even Eli's bed is bigger than the other rooms'. It's king size, with a carved wood frame and heavy, royal blue sheets. I can't help it: I picture the lump twin bed in my annex and want to carve my name into Eli's headboard..

This luxury is wasted on Eli Henderson. The stick up his ass is lodged so deep, he'll never truly relax.

I pull his desk drawers open without a murmur of guilt. Sure, he danced at the bonfire. He gripped my hips and moved us to the beat.

But then he reported me to the agency for that exact crime, trying to weasel his way out of our bet. No, I don't care if I'm invading Eli's privacy. He thinks I'm an obsessive stalker? Well, I'd hate to disappoint.

Office supplies and other loose crap jam the desk drawers. At first glance, you'd think Eli is just as orderly as Jasper, but his drawers and closet tell a different story. It's a wild tangle of clothes and books—there are local travel guides shoved in with his socks; a half-filled iron upside down in the base of his closet, leaking water onto his shoes.

Below that perfect surface, Eli is a chaotic mess.

I snap photos of everything, even though it's not exactly blackmail material.

Maybe I want to look at it later. Maybe I am a stalker.

In the bedside cabinet, I find what I'm looking for. Seems that Eli keeps tabs on his senator daddy—enough for a dossier thick with accounts of late night dinners, hotel rooms, and young female staff members.

I don't stop to dwell on what kind of fucked up family hires private investigators on each other. No doubt Senator Henderson has a matching dossier on Eli in *his* private files.

Maybe I'm even in it, thanks to that stupid party.

Honestly, it wasn't that scandalous. Senator Henderson has built a political career on *far* shadier behavior. Eli's just being a prick.

I take photos of every single page: every Polaroid, every receipt.

I don't feel good about Eli having such a creep for a dad, but I'm not sorry either. These photos are my ticket to a normal college life; my insurance against whatever else Eli throws at me this summer.

No. I'm not sorry at all.

Chapter 10

"Get your shit. We're leaving in ninety seconds."

I blink up at Nate from the pool house floor. The skirt of my maid uniform is soaked and clingy from kneeling to scrub the tiles, and wisps of hair are standing straight up from my ponytail.

"I—what?" I flatten my escaped hairs with a sweaty forearm. "I'm working, Nate."

Plus, we've barely spoken for the last week. I'm sure he forgot I exist.

Nate's eyes flick over my bucket and sponge, and the hard-bristle brush I've been working on the grout with.

"Yeah, no shit. This is work too. Sixty seconds, Layla Maid, let's go."

He strides out the door before I can argue. I could be stubborn, stay here just to piss him off, but honestly anything sounds better than scraping mold from between pool tiles. I lurch to my feet, knees pulsing as the blood flows back, and toss my brush into the bucket.

Field trip it is.

"Did you take a fucking nap?"

I slide into the passenger seat of Nate's car, only slightly out of breath, and roll my eyes. Every word Nate Becker says is halfway to a snarl and paired with constantly drumming fingertips.

"I had to change, ass hat."

The cruel slash of his mouth quirks into a grin. It's kind of funny—the ruder you are to Nate, the happier he gets.

He throws the car into gear and peels out of the driveway fast enough to spin the tires in the gravel. I keep my face blank, casually gripping the door handle like I regularly go for drives with fucking maniacs. He sneaks glances at me, the twitch in the mirrors giving him away.

I turn in my seat and face him straight on, eyebrow raised.

He grins harder.

"You always take your maids on day trips?"

Nate's father is a global sports star—a race car driver. Nate can easily keep up with the other Birchwood boys' old money. This car must be some kind of tribute, with its glossy red paint and lowered tires.

I'm not the best judge. I'd take my Toyota any day.

"Maybe I would if they were all as fucking mouthy as you."

He pushes the gear stick up a notch, his hold on it relaxed, tender. Nate drives with his whole body, leaning back and forth and stroking the steering wheel when he's thinking. My eyes snag on the thigh next to mine, strong and toned beneath his soft black jeans.

"Put your tongue away, Layla. I'm trying to drive."

For a moment, I forget that we're employer and maid. I forget that I've spent the last week avoiding him, that I resolved to blend into the wallpaper.

"Get fucked, Becker." My punch doesn't budge his muscled arm, though it cracks my knuckles.

Nate tuts, shaking his head, but his eyes glitter as they watch the road.

"If only it were that fucking easy."

The coast road bleeds into farmland, the mansions turning to barns. We watch the scenery blur past, falling into a comfortable silence as Nate drives. He flicks the radio on, rolling down his window and singing along in a surprisingly rich tenor.

He doesn't tell me where we're going, because of course he doesn't. My denim shorts and black t-shirt had better be allowed, or I'll be camping my ass out in this car.

"You've been avoiding us." When he finally speaks, it's careful. Softer than usual.

I shift on my seat, bare legs sticking to the leather. "So?"

"Is it something Eli said?"

Yes. "Of course not."

"Then what? Because he doesn't own us, you know. Jasper and me."

I clear my throat. "I could not give less of a fuck about what Eli Henderson thinks."

Nate's grip tightens on the wheel, but he doesn't call me out. Maybe he actually believes me, or maybe he just doesn't want to poke the giant elephant in the car.

"I need this job," I say at last, to break the silence more than anything. "And I need to win this bet. Anything else is a distraction."

"Didn't stop you at the bonfire."

I huff. "I wasn't on my final warning at the bonfire."

Nate shoots me a frown, eyes piercing, but all I can do is shake my head. I turn to stare out of the passenger window, throat tight.

"Thank your precious Eli for that."

Nate grumbles to himself and falls back into silence, but suddenly I'm not ready for this conversation to be over. We've never talked like this, just the two of us. I want to know how Nate works; I want to get under his skin.

"What's up with your dad?" I blurt. "How come you wound up catatonic in my bed?"

Nate turns to stone, his body rigid in the driver's seat.

"Well?"

"I drank too much."

"Yeah, okay, but why?"

"Why do you think?" Nate snarls. "The usual fucking reasons."

We both fall silent, the radio warbling a cheery little song. Nate slaps it off, and we sit there with only the purr of the engine.

"He never wanted kids," Nate says after an age. "He still doesn't. That enough information for you?"

I ignore the bite in his voice and hesitate before tracing a finger over the back of his hand. It clenches around the gear stick, but he doesn't push me away.

I don't know what else to do. What else to say. Mom and Dad have their faults, same as anyone else, but they've always loved me. Wanted me.

"You're a nosy fucker, Layla Maid."

I hum.

"Gonna use this against me?"

I shake my head. "No. Not this."

One of the other guys might bristle at the implied threat, but not Nate Becker. He shoots me a grin, eyes glittering.

"Don't hold back, Mackenzie. I fucking love when you're mean."

121

I start to tell him he needs therapy, but then we're pulling up to the sidewalk on the outskirts of a town. Run-down shop fronts line the streets, all peeling paint and boarded windows. There's a hair salon with styles in the window I haven't seen for ten years; a closed kebab shop; a Chinese takeaway with letters missing from its sign.

"So this is where the rich and famous go to unwind."

I heave my car door open, pushing out into the stale morning air. Even though the sea sparkles in the distance, the coastal breeze doesn't reach these streets. Here, the air's infused with the smell of baking concrete and last night's kebabs.

Nate strolls to the only open storefront: an ancient laundromat. My jaw drops as he pushes inside, grinning and waving to the grandma at the desk like a long-lost son.

That fucker.

"Laundry." I grit out when he emerges ten minutes later, a clothes bag folded over one arm. "You brought me on an hour-long drive to pick up your damn laundry."

Nate ignores me, laying the bag over the rear seat. His ass is impossible to look away from as he bends over, and I screw my eyes shut and pinch the bridge of my nose.

"Please tell me there's another reason. Please tell me you didn't kidnap me for an hour just to witness a single errand."

Nate smirks and slams the car door shut. "I love it when you beg."

"*Nate.* I could have done some actual work."

He places his hands on my shoulders, leans down to my eye level. "I'm sorry, Layla." He squeezes my shoulders, giving me a shake. "I didn't know you loved scrubbing grout so fucking much."

He lets go and straightens up as I sway on the spot, slipping around the car to climb back into the driver's seat. I take three tries to get my door open, my fingers scrabbling and clumsy with frustration.

"*Why*, then?" I burst out when we're nearly all the way back. Nate's fingers drum on the gear stick, his lips pressed in a tight line.

He slides me a glance and huffs out a breath, relaxing an inch.

"Figure it out, Layla. We don't have all fucking summer."

* * *

My uniform is still damp when I throw it back on and hustle to the pool house. Since Agency Georgia came calling, I scuttle between tasks like there are invisible eyes watching.

The photos on my phone mean my job is safer than ever, but I still can't relax. I don't want to give Eli grounds for a single other complaint.

It's stupid, I know. Who cares what that asshole thinks?

I barge into the pool house before I can let myself answer.

"Enjoy your field trip?"

The voice makes me jump, already wired so tight, and my strangled cry echoes around the massive room. Jasper leans against the windows, arms crossed over his chest.

I breathe out hard, pulse hammering.

It's Jasper. It's fine.

"Hardly. Becker drove me on an hour round trip to pick up his damn laundry."

Jasper blinks at me, then tosses his head back and roars with laughter, the sound bouncing around the walls and roof. Despite my best efforts, a reluctant smile tugs at my lips.

123

"That asshole," he says, tugging at a lock of his hair. "I'd have loved to see that."

"Yes, you've always preferred to torture me as a group."

Our strained history hangs unspoken in the air. The moment stretches on, and I sigh as I cross to my bucket. What did I expect exactly? An apology?

"Don't slump like that." Jasper's voice is soft, coming from close behind. "I can't bear it."

Strong arms wind around me, caging me against a firm chest, and I pluck at the rolled shirt sleeves.

"Then stop making me fucking miserable."

Jasper's sigh tickles my ear. His nose presses against my temple and slides into my hairline, my ponytail squashed against his shoulder.

"You, miserable? I'm the one who missed laundry day."

I snicker and his arms bind tighter around me. The steady thump of his heartbeat reverberates against my back, and when I press closer, I feel the hard length of him nudging my spine.

Jasper stills, breath warm on my ear.

I could die, I'm wound so tight.

"Let me go," I say, my voice ragged. His arms squeeze tighter for a split second, then unwind. I turn to face him, absorbing the heat in his eyes and the flush on his cheeks like I can commit them to memory.

Jasper's tongue darts out to wet his bottom lip.

We crash together.

He's always so tidy, so buttoned and pressed, and it is fucking delicious to rumple him. To crease his clothes and muss up his hair. I drag my hands through the wavy blond strands, twisting and scrunching it until he looks struck by lightning. And all the while, we *consume* each other, nipping and licking

124

and biting until my jaw aches. I suckle on his tongue, flooded with vicious triumph when he groans.

"How are you always so fucking *tidy*?" I pull one half of his shirt out of his pants and tug his pocket inside out for good measure.

"I like neat things," he says between bruising kisses. "They make me calm."

I bite down hard on his bottom lip and tug it with my teeth. Every perfect, orderly part of Jasper makes my feral heart surge in my chest.

"I'll make such a mess of you, Jasper Wood. I'll paint you over the walls."

I take two fistfuls of his perfect, crisp shirt and walk him back a few steps. He goes willingly, so trusting that it makes me snarl and bite his neck. I suck on the skin hard enough to bruise, and his throat bobs beneath my lips.

"I believe you." His hands map my hips, my stomach, my sides.

"You should."

I shove him into the pool.

* * *

"Please tell me you're not falling for it again."

Pierce glares at me as she peels a carrot, vicious with every swipe of the blade. She's sat on the kitchen counter, working her way through a pile of carrots and potatoes, while I lean against the fridge and beat eggs in a bowl. Diego surges back and forth between us like the waves at the beach, always grabbing, chopping, clanging.

I blow a wisp of hair from my eyes. "Falling for what,

exactly?"

Pierce rolls her eyes like I've answered her question. The boys have been wandering in and out the whole time we've been cooking, and even Eli grunted hello.

I've tried to be casual, nodding at them like it's no big deal, like they don't fluster me to high hell.

But with every awkward greeting, Pierce's eyes have narrowed more.

"They're screwing with you." Her voice rings through the kitchen as Maddox wanders in, digging behind the sofa cushions for something. "It's a joke to them. *You're* a joke to them. You know that."

Maddox's mouth presses into a firm line, but he doesn't turn around. Doesn't even acknowledge us. I wait for a moment, heel kicking against the fridge, but he doesn't deny what Pierce said.

My heart sinks.

"Maybe I'm screwing with them too."

I sound harsh, voice raw. Maddox doesn't glance over, doesn't even twitch. Just keeps digging down the back of the sofa. The clattering and hiss of the kitchen gets louder and louder until I want to press my fists into my ears and scream.

"I know what they're like," I tell Pierce instead, cool despite my thundering heart. "They showed me firsthand, all through second year. I haven't forgotten. This is all about the bet."

Maddox straightens up, taps at his recovered phone, and slips it into his back pocket. He leaves without another word, and I watch him go, gut churning.

"So long as you know when to stop."

Diego frowns at where I'm slumped against the fridge. He teases the bowl of eggs from my grip and sets it on the counter.

"You were so bouncy and smiley when you first got here. Now look at you, Layla Maid."

Pierce cocks her head, looking me over like she's just seeing me for the first time. Dark bags have taken up permanent residence under my eyes, and I know my clothes are baggier.

"Maybe it's not too late for her to swap houses."

Diego hums. "She could get some space."

I slam the whisk down on the counter, splattering raw egg everywhere.

"Can you two not discuss me like I'm not even here? Like I'm another fucking child you have to manage?"

Pierce says nothing, but I see the twitch of her eyebrow. I snarl and clutch my head, smearing raw egg into my hair.

"I'm just..." I take a deep breath, smooth my hands down the front of my dress. "I have it under control."

I whirl around and march to my annex so I don't have to see their doubting faces.

* * *

The pool water laps at my shins, cool and glittering in the moonlight. I stare down at the beads of water that catch and cling to my skin so I don't catch sight of the clock.

It's got to be almost one by now. Nearly a full hour after Maddox usually comes.

It's not like we ever said out loud that we'd meet here every night. It just sort of happened, after that first time, and now I crave our stolen time together. We just swim—even after the kiss in my galley kitchen, we haven't touched each other here.

But we share breaths and count laps, and Maddox gifts me some more of that soothing calm.

He's not coming tonight. I never really expect him to, but the rejection still stings.

The pool door scrapes open and I scramble to my feet, but the shadow that enters doesn't belong to Maddox. It's too tall, too lean.

"Come back for seconds?" I ask as Jasper steps into the moonlight.

He doesn't smile.

"A little bird tells me you're screwing with us. That you're playing with us for the bet."

He's wearing thick-framed glasses and a sweatshirt and jeans, and it makes him look younger. He walks closer, his hair sticking up at the back, like he's been tossing and turning.

"You deserve it."

Jasper watches me, close enough to touch now, his handsome face strained, then nods.

"Yes. Nicely done."

He turns to go and I snatch at his sleeve, clenching the soft fabric.

"Can't it be both? Can't I mess with you and want you at the same time?"

Jasper huffs and peels my fingers off one by one. His steady hand dwarfs mine.

"Not exactly a long-term prospect, that one."

Long term? The chlorine burns my lungs as I suck in a breath. I grab his sweatshirt again, pulling it tight across his waist, and give it a jerk.

"What if I'm not screwing with you?" I glare at Jasper's bare feet, pushing Pierce's face from my mind. "I mean, I'd sure as hell feel better about myself if I were. But what if I'm an idiot, and I really want you?"

128

The air conditioning unit rattles in the wall. I clench Jasper's sweatshirt in my damp palm.

"Are *you* messing with me?" I whisper. "If you are, this is the worst thing you've done."

It's like a statue coming to life. One moment, he's rigid, barely breathing, then he sweeps me into his arms. I let him clutch me, manhandle me, slide his hands beneath my thighs and lift me into the air. I wrap my legs around his waist and cross my ankles together.

"If I go, you go," I tell him as he walks us towards the pool.

He grins. "I'm counting on it."

Then we're weightless, and the water slams up to meet us.

I come up spluttering, my t-shirt floating around my arms. Firm hands pull it over my head and toss it on the side with a slap.

"You bastard!" I splash the back of Jasper's head as he places his glasses on top of my shirt. His hand reaches back, and he tugs his sweatshirt and t-shirt off in one pull. "For fuck's sake, Jasper. You're wearing *jeans*."

"Worth it."

He turns around and smirks, fingers popping the button open. I'm suddenly aware of my tiny bikini and bunching shorts. My fingers catch on the waistband, but then Jasper's hands cover mine.

"Let me help you with those."

He takes a breath and disappears under the water, hands burning a trail down the outside of my legs as he pulls my shorts off. When he breaks the surface, I'm more breathless than he is.

No. That smirk has to go, his face unbearably smug.

"My turn," I say, and slide his zip down before skating my

129

palms over his toned stomach.

"Down a bit."

I smack his arm and hook my fingers in his jeans before sucking in a breath. The water floods through my hair, pressing at my nose, my eyes. His jeans are stiff and unwieldy in the water, but I wrestle them down to his feet.

My eyes sting from the chlorine by the time I shoot up and gasp for air. "Next time, wear swim trunks."

Fingers smooth across my forehead, pushing my hair from my eyes. "Your feedback is noted."

We still for a moment, shivering in the cold. Water drips off his hair in streams, plunking to the surface between us. Goosebumps pebble his pale chest, his nipples hard.

"A truce?" I ask.

Jasper's hair is brown when wet. He flicks his head and droplets spray.

"You can call it that if you must."

"What would you rather call it?" I ask, breathless, as his arms wind around my waist. He pulls me flush against him.

"Must you go around labeling everything?" His hands cup my ass and squeeze. "How about a corporate reshuffling?"

I try to knee him in the balls, but he holds me too close. "So much for a long-term prospect." I push against his chest.

"Fair point." His palm rubs circles on my wriggling back and his chin rests on my head. When he speaks again, his voice is so low I have to stop thrashing so I don't miss it. "How about a fresh start?"

"Eli won't allow that." We're pressed so tight my lips touch his chest when I speak.

"Eli is not the master of the universe."

"No, but you care what he thinks."

Jasper sighs, and we both know I have him there. I should push him off, get out of the pool, and walk away from this train wreck.

My hands creep around his waist instead and flatten on his back.

"We could call it nothing." My throat is sharp when I swallow, but I force myself to keep going. "If you like. It could be our secret."

Jasper chuckles, toying with the strings on my bikini. "A secret tryst. How romantic."

I don't laugh with him. I don't think it's romantic at all. But I let him scoop me up in his arms and press me against the side of the pool. The water sloshes around us as we move together, grasping and kissing, and I rake his back with my nails to hurt him like he's hurting me.

"You've ruined me," he groans right into my mouth. His hand slides beneath my bikini top and squeezes my breast. I arch into his touch, panting. "Just like you promised. Layla, I'm fucking ruined."

I kiss him harder just to shut him up, thrusting my tongue in his mouth. I don't want to hear how I'm bad for him; I don't want to think about him keeping me a secret. I grab his hand, tug my bikini bottoms to the side, and slide his fingers over my pussy.

It's obvious, even submerged in the pool, that I'm wet for him. Aching. He curses and rubs at my entrance, then makes tight circles around my clit. I jerk in his arms, water sloshing onto the tiles, and he crowds closer, holding me still. He keeps me locked in place and works me, fingers merciless, hungry eyes boring into mine.

"Come on, Layla. Show me how much you need it."

131

His words are a cruel echo of Eli's that night, but I don't falter. I gasp and twitch my hips, riding his hand.

He slips two fingers inside me and I cry out, biting down on his shoulder.

"Look at you, desperate and moaning for me. You're fucking magnificent."

His fingers pump in and out, stroking my walls, and his thumb grinds down on my clit until my eyes blur. The tension builds and builds in my core, an unstoppable force, until I come with a groan. I spasm around his fingers as he works me through my orgasm, only slowing when I slump in his arms.

"That wasn't so terrible, was it?"

He smirks down at my bleary, flushed face. My eyes narrow, and I'm reaching for his boxers when Eli's voice calls outside.

We freeze, and the horror on Jasper's face is a punch to my gut.

"You'd better go." I unwrap my legs and step down, suddenly desperate to put some distance between us. "The master of the universe is calling."

Jasper smirks and rolls his eyes, but he climbs out of the pool. I stay in the cold water, arms crossed over my chest, watching him scoop up his clothes. He shoves the sopping jeans on, and perches his glasses on his nose. The rest he bundles under his arm, dripping onto the tiles.

"Thanks for the tryst." He winks at me. I arrange my face into a smirk.

"Find a better hiding place next time."

He waves and then he's gone, ducking out into the gardens, and I curse out my sore heart.

I don't tell myself there won't be a next time. I know it would be a lie.

Chapter 11

Three days later, Nate grabs my wrist as I'm walking across the lawn towards the gardeners' sheds.

"Let's play hide and seek."

He drags me towards the entrance of the maze, and I trip over my own feet trying to follow. Out of the corner of my eye, I notice Maddox watching us from where he's sat against a tree.

It's nothing like before, when he stared with hungry eyes as Jasper and Nate pressed me against the Bentley. Maddox's eyes narrow; his shoulders tense. Unease ripples through me and I snatch my wrist out of Nate's grip.

"I'm working, Nate."

Something like hurt flashes across the sharp planes of Nate's face, and my stomach curdles. I wrap my arms around myself and stare at the ground. Better to inspect the grass curling around my shoes than to look at him or Maddox.

"Bullshit." Nate takes hold of my wrist, but gently this time. He tugs me half a step closer, and when I look up his expression is almost pleading. "Tell me what to do, Layla Maid. You forgave Jasper, didn't you? Whatever it is, I'll do it."

I sway towards him without thinking, rocking onto my toes, arms unwinding to wrap around his shoulders. Then

133

I remember Maddox still glowering at us, and I settle back onto my heels.

When I pull my wrist away, Nate's doesn't hold on this time.

"I'm sorry," I whisper, quiet enough that only Nate can hear. I don't even know what I'm sorry for, or what I'm trying to tell him, only that I hate the way his mouth has settled back into a cruel slash.

A smile from Nate Becker is a rare thing, and a gentle smile even rarer. Now that it's gone, I'm not even sure that it really happened.

Maybe I'm projecting—seeing what I want to see. Maybe it was never like that, and Nate just wanted a willing body to have fun in the maze.

Either way, Pierce's warning rings through my head.

Nate snarls in frustration. "Stop thinking the worst of me, will you?"

He grips my face and tugs me to him, plunging his tongue into my mouth. I slant my head and cling to his shoulders, a shocked whimper sneaking between my lips. Heat floods through my body, throbbing in my core, and for a long, blissful moment I forget why I was pushing him away.

Nate Becker kisses like he drives: with his entire body, with reckless precision.

Maddox slams his book shut over by the tree, the sound echoing through the gardens, and I'm jolted out of my daze. This job, the bet, my damn pride—all of it hangs in the balance.

I'm dancing on a knife edge.

I place my palms on Nate's chest and shove him off, and he staggers back, eyes wild. My chest heaves as I watch Maddox stand up, pointedly ignoring us and brushing grass off his jeans. He walks towards the house, gait relaxed and smooth, and suddenly rage blasts through me. I barge past Nate and storm after Maddox, grabbing his shoulder and swinging him around.

"What the hell is your problem?"

Maddox raises his eyebrows, face calm, and I want to shriek.

"You didn't care if I kissed them before. What, it's no fun now I actually like them?"

Close behind me, Nate makes a noise. I ignore him, yanking Maddox's t-shirt in my grip, and a callused hand wraps over my fist.

Maddox's nostrils flare, and he spits every word between his teeth. "So you like them today? What happened to screwing with us all for the bet?"

Nate stills behind me, the sudden lack of movement deafening. I don't look back at him. I can't bear to see his face.

"Why don't you ask Jasper?" I sound desperate, even to my own ears. "He trusts me well enough."

Familiar hate swirls in Maddox's eyes, so much harder to see now than before. The breeze lifts the ends of his long brown hair, and my fingers twitch with the memory of twirling those soft strands in the grove.

How did I get here? How did I go from cradled in Maddox's lap to the cruel disdain curling his lip now? In the space of a breath, the rage drains out of me and I'm left hollow. Cold.

My grip loosens on Maddox's shirt.

"Let me go," I whisper. "Let's all just agree to leave each other alone." I sigh, finally glancing over my shoulder at Nate. "I'd lose my job, anyway. Eli saw to that."

Nate blinks at me, dumbstruck. Maddox's grip tightens on my fist, then he releases me and steps back.

"I'll be watching, Layla. Stay away from them both."

135

I nod and leave before he can say any more. I block out the raised voices behind me, throat burning.

Fuck all of this. I lock myself in the annex and don't come out for the rest of the day.

I don't even have to pretend I'm sick. No one notices I'm gone.

* * *

Jasper knocks on my door two days later. It's late: inky blackness fills the windows. I've started locking myself in when I retreat to the annex each night.

I don't know why. It's not like they're messing with me anymore. We are employers and maid. I clean the house and help the other staff, and they disappear for most of the day.

If Nate and Jasper find me working, if they try to catch my eye, I pretend not to notice. And if Maddox or Eli smile at each other, darkly satisfied, I pretend not to see that too.

Whatever. I'm here for the payout, not to heal old wounds.

And I don't care if Eli's stopped trying to break me: he owes me that damn money.

It's harder to ignore Jasper knocking at my annex door, but I do. I leave him outside.

He knocks, and I sit on my twin bed, knees tucked under my chin, willing my chest to stop aching. And when he calls my phone, I switch it off and stuff it under the pillow.

Nate knocks the next night, battering my annex, louder and more insistent than Jasper. He tries the door attached to the mansion first, then storms into the gardens and thumps on the back entrance, the windows. I curl up on the hallway floorboards, out of sight, and put my headphones in.

Nate doesn't call me. And he doesn't knock again after that.

"This is a good thing!" Pierce's tinny voice echoes from my handset. "Now you can have the summer you came here for. No Birchwood boys, no dramas: just sunshine, surfing, a monster payout, and maybe a guy who doesn't hate your guts."

"No kidding." My lips feel numb as I speak. "Surfing tomorrow before work?"

It's fun—the icy sting of salt water, the whooping when we stand up—but even the pink blush of sunrise doesn't stir me. It's like I'm seeing it all, living it all, behind a pane of glass.

When we collapse into the sand, wetsuits pooled around our waists, Pierce's grin stretches her cheeks. My own face is lifeless, and I force my lips into a smile.

It's more of a grimace, judging by how a passing dog walker tugs her puppy away.

I stop pretending. My face settles back into a calm mask.

Pierce gusts out a sigh. "What is it, Layla? Tell me how we can fix this."

I shrug, winding my arms around my knees. I can't tell Pierce why I'm hurting so much, why my chest aches so much I can't catch my breath.

I can't even admit it to myself.

"Just in a weird mood, I guess. It'll pass." She grunts, unconvinced, and I muster up a proper smile, nudging her with my elbow. "Surfing was fun. I kicked your ass."

Pierce snorts, and then we're on to other things: the tear in her new wetsuit; the fancy synchronized swimming lessons her guest family's kids have twice a week.

I nod and murmur in all the right places, determined to stop her worrying.

Finally, it's Eli who takes me by the elbow while I'm vacu-

137

uming the upstairs hallway. He drags me into the empty study, the vacuum dropped and whirring on the rug.

The door clicks shut behind us, dulling the noise to a low hum. I glance around at the shelves of leather-bound books and waxy houseplants with disinterest.

"Layla."

Eli's voice cracks like a whip. I turn my head to him slowly.

"What's going on with you? Did someone..." He swallows, licks his lips. "Has someone hurt you?"

I frown at the guy who made my life at college hell, who humiliated me over and over. Who offered forty thousand dollars for the joy of torturing me through the summer.

"Other than you, you mean."

My voice is flat, and he flinches.

"I did this, then?" Eli's voice is hoarse. Distantly, it occurs to me that I've never seen him this pale. "I pushed you too far."

My shoulders hitch up, then collapse. "Wasn't that the whole point?"

I turn to go, but Eli steps in my way.

"I thought maybe... things were getting better. Between the two of us. Between all of us."

"Yes." I frown at him. "And then you tried to get rid of me."

He's shaking his head before I've even finished talking. He steps closer, running gentle hands up the bare skin of my arms.

"I didn't report you, Layla. That wasn't me."

I shake my head. None of this makes any sense. "I came to you. You told me you did it."

And it's true: I stood in his bedroom and tore into Eli, hungry for blood.

He squeezes my upper arms, gives me a quick shake. "I never said that, Layla. I hurt you, yes. I made that stupid bet. But I

138

didn't report you, I swear. I *want* you to win, Layla. I have for a while. I'm rooting for you."

Sounds like a dumb way to spend forty thousand dollars, but that's none of my business.

I nod and step around him, still hollow and numb, and Eli lets out a growl. He snatches me to his chest, pressing his warm body against mine. I let him, arms dangling like a rag doll, and Eli's chest heaves with frustration.

"Tell me what this is about, Layla." His cheek presses to the side of my head. "Please. Let me fix it for you."

I swallow, tears brimming behind my eyes, and I hate that he's done that. I hate that he's pulled me out of my comfortable numbness, and the first thing I feel again is pain.

"I'm just tired," I whisper to his collarbone. "Of all of it. The fighting and the accusations. I'm tired of being pulled between the four of you like a toy. Even when one of you wants me, the others bleed me for it."

I shrug out of his arms, stepping back to smooth the creases from my dress. I blink hard and my cheeks stay dry.

Good. I'm getting stronger.

"Layla." Eli's voice cracks. His hand reaches for me, and I watch it until it drops.

"Two more weeks, Eli. Then I take your money, and we go back to campus. Leave me alone next year, okay?"

He nods, jaw clenched, and it's the first flutter of hope I've had all week.

* * *

My arms cut through the water, my head tilting to one side to breathe. I pull myself forward with powerful strokes, arms and shoulders burning.

I'm faster than six weeks ago. Stronger. I barely register the body slipping into the deep end of the pool, feet treading water.

It's not Maddox. Even out of the corner of my eye, even through the curtains of bubbles, I know his form by heart. This body is leaner, more slender, and it stays at the deep end like it's waiting for me.

I fold my arms onto the tiles and peel my goggles off. They leave angry red circles on my skin, but I don't care. I suck in a few gasping breaths and turn to Diego.

"Nice, huh?"

I've been needling him for weeks to sneak into the pool house after hours. He works so hard for the agency, catering brunches and luncheons, then coming here for the last meal of the day. He, more than anyone, deserves some extra perks.

Diego smirks at my goggle marks and wet mop of hair.

"Glad you've made yourself at home, Layla Maid."

I stick my tongue out and he laughs.

It's so easy with Diego. So carefree. There's no metric ton of baggage, no mistrust and pain. I don't have that with anyone else, not even Pierce any more. Not with the suspicion prickling under my skin.

We mess about like two kids, holding races and handstand competitions. We're in the middle of a diving competition when the pool door opens, cool night air gusting over the tiles. Diego comes up, spluttering and cursing from a belly flop, while I howl with laughter.

The mirth drains from my face when I see Maddox standing in the doorway. He watches us, eyes darting between Diego and my bikini-clad body. I cross my arms below my chest, suddenly self-conscious, and quickly slide back into the pool.

It's better once I'm back in the water, my body blurred and warped.

Maddox could get us both fired for this. Diego must know that, but he grins and tips his chin up at him like they're old friends.

"Hey, man. Coming in? Layla Maid has a mean cannonball."

Maddox pulls back half a step, and I can breathe again. He's not staying: good. I don't want him here. If he reports us, I'll take the blame.

"Sure." Maddox's smoky voice makes my toes scrunch. "I'm game."

He kicks off his shoes and leaves his pile of clothes right by the door. Our stuff is closer to the edge, soaking wet from our games. I look away when he pulls his shirt off, staring out the giant windows like I'm suddenly fascinated by the moonlit gardens.

Even without looking, I feel his body slide into the water. It's impossible, I know it is, but I swear his heat reaches me across the pool, warming my skin and spreading over my shaking limbs.

Maddox, oh-so-serious Maddox, joins in with our nonsense games. Diego takes charge, since I've clammed up and gone silent. He directs us through races, times us treading water, even tries to teach us the butterfly. Maddox picks it up straight away, the powerful muscles on his back flexing, but I flop around like a dying fish.

I come up spluttering, the pool house ringing with their laughter, but for once Maddox is smiling, not cruel.

"I'm more of a breaststroke girl," I say without thinking, and nearly die at the way his eyes heat. I whip my eyes back to

141

Diego, splashing the laughing chef, and leap onto his back.

It's Diego who makes the first move to leave, and I shoot out of the pool on his heels. The last person in the world I want to be alone with is Maddox Landry. But Diego grunts and pokes at his soaked clothes with his toe, scooping them up without bothering to get dressed.

"I'll see you both tomorrow," he says, throwing me a wink, before sliding out of the door. I'm left half dressed, a towel wrapped around my shoulders as I cram my feet into my shoes.

There's a rush and splatter of water as Maddox pushes himself from the pool. I snatch blindly for what's left of my stuff.

"Layla, wait."

Warm fingers trail down my arm, and I reel back, nearly tripping onto a sun lounger. Maddox watches me, mouth turned down, hair dripping down his broad chest.

"I haven't gone near them," I snap. "Any of them. You can save your threats."

Maddox frowns, and I skirt around him, keeping my distance as I make way to the door.

"That's not what I was going to say," he calls, but I don't slow down. I don't breathe until I'm safe in the night air.

* * *

"The agency received another complaint. About Miss Mackenzie's conduct."

Georgia flicks her eyes over me, lips pursed, as I stand between her and Eli in the marble lobby. My hands twitch to smooth my uniform, but I clasp them behind my back instead.

Georgia raises her eyebrows, but I say nothing. I haven't

spoken a word since Eli summoned me to the lobby.

What's the point? She's already decided what she thinks of me, and nothing I say will change that.

And it doesn't matter what the complaint is—whether Maddox complained about the pool, or someone else wants me fired. It doesn't even matter if the complaint is true: my final warning is gone.

I hope it's about the pool. At least I'm guilty of that one. And while I've doubtlessly had some *unprofessional* moments with each of the boys, they were equally to blame.

"I'm not sure why. We've found Layla to be an exemplary worker."

Georgia's eyebrows shoot up her forehead, and I can't keep the shock from my face. I quickly smooth my face blank again, but I know Eli saw. He's been watching me intently since I walked into the room, barely sparing Georgia a glance.

She tugs on her blazer sleeve, glancing between us. "Mr Henderson, someone has filed a second complaint. Perhaps one or more of the guests reached out without mentioning it to you. And as you are already aware, Miss Mackenzie is on her final warning. You yourself wanted a different maid when you arrived."

Eli doesn't like that. The look he shoots Georgia is pure venom.

"Layla has done an excellent job. Is this how the agency treats its dedicated employees?"

It's weird watching Eli Henderson go to bat for me. I knew as soon as I saw Georgia—standing to attention in the lobby like an executioner in heels—my summer job is over. And sure, it hurts, but I'm still comfortably numb, going through my days wrapped up in cotton wool.

143

Plus, as far as I'm concerned, I've won the damn bet. Otherwise this was all for nothing, and I can't stand that. Eli can pay up while I pack.

"The decision is made," Georgia snaps, her decorum sliding for a moment. She huffs and tugs on her sleeve again, rearranging her frown into a calm smile.

"This is a courtesy visit. Your replacement maid will be here within the hour. Miss Mackenzie, here is your paperwork."

The paper folder slaps into my palm. I take it, ears ringing.

It doesn't matter, not really. It's just a fucking job, and with the money from the bet, I'll hardly be homeless. There are only ten more days left of summer, then this nightmare will be behind me.

Still, one thought pulses in my head: *I got fired. I got fired. I got fired.* Suddenly, I'm being kicked out of my dorm again; I'm losing my gallery internship. Every time I let my guard down with these guys, the universe punishes me for it.

I truly hate them right now.

The noises of the house fade back in, along with Eli's clipped voice.

"We've rented the house in its entirety, correct?"

Georgia cocks her head. "Well, yes, of course."

He turns to me, anger fading to concern. "Pack up your things, Layla. Pick whichever guest bedroom you like."

Georgia splutters, and the two of them start arguing again. I leave them to it, drifting through the halls to my sweet little annex.

It was mine for a while, there. My haven. My port in the Birchwood boy storm.

I could fight Eli for the sake of it, insist on finding a motel, but honestly I'm too damn exhausted. We've managed over

144

six weeks together; we'll survive ten more days.

I take vicious pleasure in dragging my ratty zebra print hold-all past Georgia in the lobby. Her hand twitches towards her throat, and I swear she nearly gags.

Good. My bag thumps against each step, all the way to the top, and when I swing around to address the lobby like some kind of duchess, Eli fights a smirk.

"Let me know when the new maid arrives. I'd like her to turn down my room."

With a final nasty smile at Georgia, I swan down the hallway, my hold-all catching on the rug.

Chapter 12

The new maid is called Katerina: a sunny, plump woman in her thirties with brown skin and glossy black hair. She throws her head back and cackles when I tell her I don't really need anything—I was making a point.

"You tell 'em, honey. They've been nothing but cold to you."

I guess gossip travels fast.

Even though I keep telling her not to worry, Katerina helps me move the last of my things over and straightens out my room with me. Her eyebrows start in a normal place above her eyes and drift steadily higher as each of the guys checks in on me.

"I'm so sorry, Layla." Jasper squeezes the door frame, lingering on the threshold like he's afraid to step inside.

Nate, on the other hand, barges in without knocking, the door bouncing off the wall.

"This is bullshit," he snarls, and I shrug. It's true. But I grab his hand and squeeze it, and his shoulders drop an inch.

"Don't fuck up my new room, Becker. I'm giving the high life a try."

Even Maddox knocks gently and rakes his gaze over me, before nodding and drifting away.

Katerina's smile is sly as she pushes the window open, letting the ocean breeze in. The water sparkles turquoise in the distance, and tiny people move like ants across the sand.

"Inappropriate conduct, huh? My, my."

I snort. "Hardly. They're not as nice as they look."

Katerina bumps me with her hip on her way to the door. "That just makes it better."

I wait until I'm finally, blissfully alone, before I pull out my phone. A horrible suspicion curdles in my gut, and I need to banish this stupid thought from my mind.

"Hey girl! We on for surfing later?"

Pierce doesn't *sound* like she just got me fired, and hope flares bright in my chest.

"It's done. There was another complaint." My throat is tight. "I got fired."

A sharp intake of breath whistles down the phone.

"Oh my God."

I scrunch my eyes up, hating myself for even wondering, completely lost with how to even ask. But in the end, I don't have to. She doesn't make me.

It's clear in her voice.

"Lay, I... I never thought they'd fire you. I thought they'd move you to another house."

I nod even though she can't see, eyes screwed shut and tears spilling down my cheeks. The bed is soft when I sink onto it, and I grind the heel of my palm into one eye.

"It was you before, too."

It's not a question. Eli told me it was none of the guys and I believe him.

Pierce's whisper is so quiet I almost miss it.

"Yes."

"*Why?*"

I'm being too loud, I know I am. Someone will hear.

"They're not good for you, Lay. You've been so unhappy. And this ridiculous bet—you deserve so much better."

"And getting me fired is better?"

"No!" Pierce starts to cry too. My heart throbs in my chest. "I thought since there's no proof, the agency would move you somewhere else and you could have the summer you wanted."

I grit my teeth. "You lied to me, Pierce. You went behind my back."

It's a long time before she speaks again.

"I knew that no matter what they did, you'd want to stay with them. You're addicted, Lay. Even last year, you couldn't keep away."

I end the call before she can say any more.

I don't want to hear it.

* * *

Eli finds me after dinner, curled up on the window seat watching the sea. We're close enough to see the white froth of the breakers, and I've been watching the surfers with my chin resting on my folded arms.

Dusk is in full view on this side of the house. It's so beautiful, it's like a punch to the gut. I've seen the sunset from the gardens, but not from this high up. Not like this. The sky bleeds crimson to orange to pink, and the ocean shimmers silver.

"It's beautiful."

Eli pads across the rug and into my peripheral vision. He's dressed down: a plain white t-shirt and soft blue jeans. He folds his arms and takes in the view with me.

"Yes. It is."

We stay there for a long time, sharing breaths, until the molten sun dips below the horizon. When Eli turns to me, blue-tinged shadows fill the room.

"Layla…"

I hold up a palm and unfold myself from the window seat. It brings me into his space, into arm's length, but neither of us reach for the other.

"I need to show you something."

My phone takes a minute to wake up. I knock it against the windowpane and push down the prickle of embarrassment, and when the screen finally glows to life, I pull up the photos.

"They're from before," I tell him, handing the phone over. Eli plucks it from my shaking hand. "When I thought you were trying to back out of the bet. They were… insurance, I guess."

Eli's mouth tightens when he sees the first photo—the first page of his father's file. As his thumb swipes through the photos, he gradually turns to stone.

After the last photo, he hands my phone back without a word.

"You can delete them." I offer it up. "I already got rid of the back-ups."

Eli glares at my phone but doesn't take it again. "Then why show me at all?"

I sigh and turn to show him the screen as I delete them all, one by one.

"Not telling you felt like lying."

"And?"

His voice is rough. Eli's spoiling for a fight. I delete the last photo, flick through my gallery to show him, then toss my

149

phone on my bed.

"And I don't want to lie. Not to you."

The cold flowing off him is so much worse now I've felt his heat. His jaw ticks when I step closer.

"I meant it the night I kissed you."

It hurts more to admit than I thought it would. I paid for that party so many times over.

It would almost be easier if I *had* set him up. Instead, I kissed a guy I liked, fooled around with him in a cloakroom, then suffered his wrath for a year.

The worst part was always that Eli blamed me. That he didn't fucking notice just how far gone I was for him. I wanted him that night, and I've wanted him every night since, and I tell him so.

"Don't." His voice is ragged, and he reaches up to trace his thumb over my lip. "Please don't. I can't bear it, Layla."

I swallow, mouth shifting beneath his thumb. "Why not?"

Misery swirls in his eyes.

"Because if that's true, I ruined the best thing that ever happened to me. I tortured the only girl I've ever wanted, and all for the crime of wanting me back."

My eyelashes flutter shut, and I let his words flow through me. *He wanted me, he wanted me, he wanted me.*

I haven't been as alone as I'd thought.

When I look up at him again, a smile lifts my cheeks. He watches it hungrily, and when I suck his thumb into my mouth, his pupils blow wide.

"Fuck." It's half groan, half hiss, and I swirl my tongue over the pad of his thumb. I slide my lips over his knuckle and scrape my teeth against his skin on the way back.

"I thought..." Eli frowns, fighting to concentrate as I let his thumb go with a wet pop. "I thought I'd lost you, Layla. I thought one of the others—Jasper or Nate…"

Right. This isn't as straightforward as a year ago. If I admit I want his friends too, I could lose him all over again.

But I meant it when I said that I'm done with the lies.

"I…"

The words are there, but they jumble up in my mouth. I place my hand on Eli's firm chest, warmth seeping through his thin t-shirt, and bunch the fabric in my fist. It anchors me, and he cups my elbow before I say the next words.

"I want you, but I want them, too. All of them, Eli."

For a moment, he stills, shock rippling over his face. Then he blows out a long breath, his grip tightening on my elbow.

"I never thought I'd be into something like that."

Eli gives me a rueful smile and tugs me against him. The evidence of just how interested he is presses against my stomach.

"Just us four?" His nose tracks over my temple and into my hair. I nod, shivers skating down my spine. "No others, Layla."

His last words are a proclamation. Laying down the law. My core clenches at the dominance in his tone.

"No others," I agree, trailing off into a moan and Eli nips at my earlobe. My hands roam over his chest, his waist, his hard stomach.

A hand fists my hair and tugs my head to the side.

"Good girl," Eli murmurs, teeth scraping the pulse point in my neck. My legs go weak beneath me, and he holds me firm at the hip. "Not yet, though."

Eli walks me backwards until I'm pressed against the wall.

"I want you first."

Over his shoulder, the warm light of the hallway spills

through the crack of the open door. Anyone could walk in on us. Anyone could walk past and see. The thought makes me moan and buck against his hold.

"Enough."

The command tears through me, and I still, chest heaving. I'm slick and swollen in my panties, so wet it's sliding down my thigh. Eli reads the desperation written on my face and growls.

"Tell me what you need, Layla."

My reply is immediate. "I need to come."

Eli's mouth quirks and I strain for it, but he pushes me back against the wall. "Be more specific. Do you want to ride my hand?"

His fingers trace between my breasts, over my stomach, and down over my shorts. They rub over my pussy, a barely there tease, and I whine and thrust my hips.

He toys with me, letting me chase his hand then pulling it away. Finally, he rubs harder, the seam of my shorts pressing into my clit. I groan and thunk my head against the wall.

"No," Eli murmurs and takes his hand away. My chest heaves for breath, for oxygen, and I could weep from frustration. "No, you already came on Jasper's hand."

"How did you…" I can't even finish the thought, but it doesn't matter. Eli drops to his knees in front of me, and my brain short-circuits.

Even on his knees, there is no question of who's in charge. Eli's palm smooths up my thigh, firm and sure, and his eyes bore into mine as he flicks the button of my shorts open.

"You're going to ride my face, Layla." He says it casually, like we're talking about the weather. "You're going to work your pussy on my tongue, and only once you've shown me how much you need it am I going to give you my cock."

I whimper, nodding frantically as he tugs my zipper down. Yeah. That works for me.

My shorts hit the floorboards and I step out of them on wobbly legs. Eli hooks his fingers through my panties, but then leans forward and seals his mouth over the soaked lace. His tongue lathes the fabric, right along my seam, and I gasp, legs twitching already.

Eli growls in approval and yanks my panties down, helping me step out of them before sealing his mouth to me again. There's nothing between us this time, no barrier between the hot slide of his tongue and my swollen pussy. He laps and lathes at me, fingers bruising my hips, before finding the tight bundle of nerves and sucking at my clit.

I let out a yell, arching away from the wall, and grabbing fistfuls of his black hair. He slides one arm beneath my thigh and tosses a leg over his shoulder, opening me up to him and grinding his nose and chin into my slick heat.

When his tongue slides back over my pussy and probes at my opening, I hold him tight and move my hips. His grip on me doesn't falter—he urges me on, dares me to go faster.

This won't be a leisurely fuck. We've both wanted this for too long.

Eli's tongue slides inside me, stroking my inner walls, and I moan loud and long. I ride his face, smearing my wetness all over his nose and chin, not caring that I'm losing control.

"Do you want it, Layla?"

He's ragged, ruined, as he pulls his mouth away. Two thick fingers slide inside me, reaching deeper than his tongue could.

"Yes," I grunt, still tugging on his hair. "Fuck, yes."

He shrugs my leg off his shoulder and stands up, wiping his

153

forearm over his chin. When he scoops me up and presses me into the wall, I wrap my legs around his waist.

The rough denim of his jeans scrapes over my aching pussy and makes me squirm.

"Hurry." I urge him on, grabbing two fistfuls of t-shirt as he unbuttons his jeans and shoves them down his hips. "Please, Eli. I need it. Hurry."

"Shh." His forehead rests against mine, both of us hot and sweating. His cock is huge and flushed in his palm, jutting towards me as he rolls on a condom. "Such a good girl."

He lines up against my entrance and presses inside, slow but firm. I tuck my head against the side of his neck, toes curling.

"Fuck. Eli, fuck."

He bottoms out, sealing us tight together, and we both let out a groan.

"You're mine." He thrusts: shallow at first, then harder, deeper. I tilt my hips to take every inch of him, jerking up to meet him. "Do you understand me, Layla? Mine."

I nod, too out of my mind to speak, and lick a stripe up his neck instead. He pounds into me, hard enough to rattle my teeth together, and I take every glorious inch of his cock. Pleasure sparks and hums through my veins, gathering in my aching core.

A bead of his sweat drips onto my cheek, and I swipe my tongue out to taste it. I want every single part of him; I want his scent stamped on me like a brand. I want him to seal us so tightly together that we'll never come fully undone.

He shifts my weight against the wall, then his palm cracks against my ass. Heat blooms over my skin, sharpening the pleasure throbbing in my pussy.

"Fuck, yes." I bite down hard on his neck, sucking up a bruise.

Eli grunts and pounds into me harder, his flesh slapping into mine.

"You're so gorgeous squirming on my cock, Layla. You take it so well, baby. Your pussy is perfect."

Eli mutters into the side of my face, then captures my mouth with his. He tugs my bottom lip between his teeth just as his thumb skates over my clit. He rubs quick, tight circles over the bundle of nerves until I'm shuddering against the wall, wound to breaking point.

"Fuck!"

I arch against him, pussy clamping down on his cock. Shock waves roll through me, surge after surge of pleasure, and I let out a wail.

Dimly, I notice Eli tense and swell inside me. He groans and mutters a string of curses as he comes inside my pussy, our bodies sealed tight.

We stay locked that way for several long minutes, my head pressed against his neck, our chests heaving for breath. Finally, Eli slides himself out of me and sets me on my feet.

I stumble a little, legs like jelly, and he sets me on the window seat. After ducking into the en suite to deal with the condom, he comes back with a warm, damp cloth.

"You look like nothing happened."

I can't hide the bitterness in my voice. Eli's tucked away and buttoned, his clothes smoothed and his hair flattened. The only sign that he hasn't just been sitting at a desk is the flush on his cheeks and the light sheen of sweat.

That, and the bruise I sucked into his neck. I trace it with my fingertips as he kneels in front of me and wipes the cloth gently over my sore pussy.

Eli huffs a laugh. "Yes, thank you for that."

155

I shrug, unrepentant. "You're not the only one who wants to stake a claim."

His gaze is smoldering, his face smug as he rises and tosses the cloth into the laundry basket.

"Come on." He gathers my panties and shorts and drops them in my lap. "You're our guest, now. No more hiding in your room."

I grumble but get dressed, buttoning my shorts.

And even though a voice in my head screams at me to stop, I can't help but say: "This better not have been about the bet, Eli."

As soon as the words are out in the air, I wish I could take them back. What just happened between us was real, I *know* it was, but a year's patterns are hard to break.

The scathing look Eli throws me would strip paint from the walls.

"Forget the damn bet. I paid you over a week ago. Have you never heard of online banking?"

Huh. Guess I really am an idiot.

I'll make it up to him later. I already have some ideas.

* * *

The guys are in the rec room: a vast upstairs room that's double the size of my whole annex. Well, Katerina's annex, I guess. Even though my new bedroom is objectively nicer, the loss of my haven still stings.

Plush Turkish rugs cover polished oak floorboards, and squat leather sofas are scattered through the room. A home cinema screen perches on one wall, and a giant pool table with spotlights takes pride of place.

We've been here together once before: after the party, when Jasper and Maddox helped me clean.

Part of me wonders if they picked this room to soften me up.

Eli leads me through a corner doorway, and he must sense the nerves buzzing in my stomach because he pulls me by the hand to the bar. I slide onto a stool and watch Jasper, Nate, and Maddox play poker across the room.

They've dragged three armchairs around a coffee table, hitching up folds in the rugs. Their necks are bent, the concentration thick in the air.

Eli clears his throat. He flicks a dish towel over one shoulder and leans both hands on the wood of the bar. The smile quirking the corner of his mouth is pure sin.

"What will it be, miss?"

I manage not to fan myself, craning my neck to see the fridges behind him. They're lined with row after row of bottles: ciders and beers and spirits. I can tell they're expensive: I don't recognize a single label, for a start, and the glass of the bottles seems thick. Substantial.

"I, uh." I scrunch up my nose. "Something with rum?"

It comes out like a question, and while yesterday I couldn't have cared less what Eli thought of my drink choices, now that he's being nice, I'm weirdly self-conscious.

"An excellent choice, miss. Very beach-appropriate."

Eli ignores the fridges and slides a heavy bottle off the shelf. It's two-thirds full of amber liquid and shaped like something out of a pirate film. He mixes two cocktails like a pro, and I watch his precise, steady movements with lust curling in my belly.

He handled my body with the same confident ease. I squeeze

my thighs together and shift on my stool.

"Is this a detente?"

Jasper's palm on my back makes me jump. He's not quite touching me, hovering a hair's breadth away from my skin, but somehow that tickle of heat makes me squirm even more.

Eli watches me with a knowing smirk.

I open my mouth and shut it again, the recent memory of Eli plunging inside me and fucking me against a wall rendering me stupid.

"Something like that," Eli says. He sets a cocktail down in front of me, condensation beading the glass. The drink is a deep blackcurrant color, with a slice of orange speared over the rim.

"Thanks," I choke out, and take a hurried gulp while Jasper looks between us with renewed interest. It's delicious: sweet and tart with hints of ginger, and I cradle the glass to my chest as Eli leads us across the room to the others.

Maddox and Nate are locked in some kind of showdown. They glare at the cards held tight in their hands, shooting assessing glances at each other. Maddox's fingers drum against his knee, while Nate lounges back in his armchair like he might fall asleep at any minute.

"Well, *someone* make a goddamn move," Jasper says as we arrive. Both guys glance over at us, then straighten an inch in their chairs.

Maddox looks back at his cards, frowning. But Nate stares at where I'm hovering awkwardly between Jasper and Eli.

I raise a hand, giving a stupid little wave. "Um, hi."

Nate tosses his cards down. "Fold."

Maddox scoffs but scoops up the rest of the pack, shuffling them without looking. Heat curls in my belly again, but I don't kid myself with Maddox.

Nate stares at me with hungry eyes. Jasper finds any excuse to touch me. And Eli—Eli has made his feelings about me pretty damn clear.

Maddox was the first of the Birchwood boys to give me another chance. And now he's the one who wishes I would leave.

It shouldn't hurt—three gorgeous guys should be enough, Layla—but it does.

The silence stretches out, heavy and awkward, and I take another gulp of my drink. It burns my throat, but I don't care. I'd swim in it, it tastes so good, and at least then I'd be away from the tension clouding this room.

I could leave. Eli, Jasper and Nate might complain, but I know none of them would stop me. I could slip away with my tail between my legs and finish my drink in my room.

No. I don't think so.

I slide onto the arm of Nate's chair, directly opposite Maddox.

"What are we playing?"

Nate's arm winds around my hips, fingers stroking my bare thigh. I shiver and bite my lip, catching Eli's eye for a second and matching his smirk with one of my own. I pivot on the arm of the chair, the leather squeaking against my bare skin, and tuck my feet under Nate's leg.

His dark eyes burn into mine, tension radiating through his frame. We stare at each other, his fingers tracing faster and faster patterns into my skin, until an amused chuckle from Jasper tugs me back to reality.

"A new game, it seems," Jasper murmurs, almost to himself.

Then he swaps a wicked grin with Eli and the temperature

in the room soars. The gentle trace of fingertips on my thigh becomes the slide of a hand. My toes curl under Nate's legs and he must feel it, because he huffs a laugh and tugs me fully into his lap.

Cradled between strong, muscled thighs, with my back pressed to his chest, Nate's sweatpants do nothing to hide the hard length of him pressed against my spine. My breath hitches when I feel it and I press back harder, rubbing along him just a fraction of an inch.

Nate groans like I reached into his boxers and jerked his cock. Jasper shifts forward in his chair, elbows braced on his knees as he watches us. Eli sips his drink like he's in some gentleman's club, swirling the liquid in the glass.

And Maddox, he places the cards on the table and leaves without a word.

His broad shoulders are tense under his long-sleeved shirt, and he drags a hand through his long brown hair as he crosses the room. I watch him go, my heart sinking all the way through the floorboards to the house's foundations.

Nate keeps stroking my leg, nuzzling at my neck, but the heat that burned in me only a moment ago has snuffed out. The cold way Maddox looked at me—the way his mouth turned down. A chill spreads through me, and I slide out of Nate's lap and onto a separate chair.

"Deal me in," I mutter, refusing to meet any of their eyes.

They shift in their seats, Nate cursing Maddox out under his breath, but Jasper scoops up the cards and deals us our first hand with efficient flicks of his wrist.

"Ace high."

The rest of his introduction washes over my head. I take another gulp of my rum cocktail, savoring the burn at the back of my throat.

It's nothing new to me—rejection from one of the Birchwood boys. But somehow it's worse when the others have come around; when I let myself hope I could win them all.

Suddenly my proclamation to Eli that I wanted all four feels like the worst kind of hubris. Humiliation stains my cheeks red, and I sink deeper into my chair.

Chapter 13

Without Maddox on board, it doesn't feel right to mess around with Jasper and Nate. Not because I need his permission, or anything like that. But because even though he's now pretending I don't exist, falling silent when I enter a room and leaving if I make myself comfortable, I don't want the asshole to feel pushed out. He was here first, after all.

Whatever. I know it's ridiculous. I can practically hear what Pierce would say, if I finally called her back.

"Why the hell are you feeling sorry for him? That fucker deserves it! Screw his friends right in front of him!"

I almost call her, too, just to hear that righteous anger, my thumb hovering over the call button more times than I can count. But then I remember the way Georgia looked at me: like I was a cockroach infesting the beach house.

Pierce did that. The girl who stood by me when no one else did, who made second year of college bearable—she did that to me.

I'm not going to throw away years of friendship over one mistake. Not even this fucking stinker of one. I messaged her to say that, a few days after our call, but I also said I needed time.

She listened. Pierce hasn't tried to call or message me once since.

I'm not sure if that makes me feel better or worse.

Eli still slips into my room at night, and pulls me into alcoves and hidden corners throughout the day. I savor every kiss, every touch, every groan we release into each other's mouth like they're a balm to my soul.

For the first few days after Maddox walked out, I half expected Eli to tease me about my failed play for his friends.

He doesn't, though. If anything, he seems almost as frustrated as I am. He watches me joke around with Nate or curl up next to Jasper when we watch a film with a frown creasing his forehead.

Like he can see everything this *could* be. Everything it was meant to be.

I know that frustration. It's why I make a point not to touch either of them, always leaving a gap between us on the couch. I don't want to torment myself with what could have been, what I stupidly wanted.

"He'll come around."

Eli toys with my hair as we sprawl on the grass. My head rests on his lap, his fingers raking through my dark waves. Nate and Jasper lie nearby, Jasper reading a worn paperback and Nate silent with an arm tossed over his eyes.

I can't tell if he's brooding or taking an angry nap, but I know it's not worth the fallout to ask.

"I don't think so."

We don't have to spell out who we're discussing. There's no one else with a grudge against me left. Nate and Jasper pretend not to listen, but Jasper hasn't turned his page for several minutes.

163

"He's liked you for years," Eli says. "He liked you before we hooked up at that party."

"Seriously?"

I squint up at Eli, but the sun is right behind his head. It seems impossible; Maddox Landry didn't know I existed until I pissed off his friend. I used to seek out the contagious calm of his presence, sitting near him to read in the quad, and not once did he say hello.

Eli shrugs, looking almost guilty.

"He was going to ask you out."

I look away and listen to the breeze shiver through the trees, processing this fresh information. After a while, I snort and dig my elbow into his side.

"Some friend you are."

Nate flings his arm off his face. "Tell us about it."

I roll off Eli's lap and crawl over to Nate, stopping when my face hovers above his. I haven't pushed it like this since the poker night, but Eli's confession has made my chest bloom with fresh hope.

"Oh, Nate. Does the poor little rich boy feel left out?"

He bares his teeth and grabs my shoulders, launching up and rolling us until I'm the one pressed into the grass.

This jackass. He fucking loves when I'm mean to him.

"The poor rich boy *is* left out."

"Rich *boys*," Jasper corrects, turning his page.

Nate's eyes glitter down at me, and very deliberately, he rolls his hips into mine. It's a challenge. We've danced around this all fucking summer, and I'm as sick of waiting as he is. I turn my head and find Eli watching me, fierce approval written over his face.

"Come on." I push Nate off and he goes easily, tipping to one side. I grab his tattooed wrist as I stand up, and nudge Jasper with my toe. "Show me this maze you like so much."

"Make sure you show her more than plants," Eli says idly. He plucks Jasper's abandoned book up and flips it over to read the back.

My heart thunders in my rib cage as I lead them to the maze entrance, and I march faster so I don't have time to overthink. Images of getting caught fill my mind, it's that doomed party with Eli all over again—

"Do the gardeners come in here?" I wonder aloud as Jasper takes the lead, guiding us through the narrow pathway between hedges.

Nate snorts, his wrist still gripped tight in my hand. "No, Layla. It grows like this."

I shove him shoulder-first into the hedge, and our bickering soothes me as Jasper leads us around a corner. The path stops a few feet away. A dead end.

"Did you forget the way?"

Jasper smirks and tugs me further down the path. "Less likely to get caught off-route."

The hedge walls tower overhead, birds rustling in their tangled branches. The sounds of the garden—the crash of distant waves, the rumble of cars driving along the lane—they fade away.

It's quiet in here. Cool; untouched by the sun. I cross my arms to hide my stiff nipples.

Our footsteps scuff the scraggly grass. I take a deep breath, then push the two guys shoulder-to-shoulder.

They may have their own ideas, but I know exactly what I want to do. I've thought about it every day since they caged me in at that bonfire.

Nate lets out a hiss as I drop to my knees. I fumble with Jasper's belt, smacking Nate's hands away when he reaches to slide down his dark sweatpants.

I want to do it. I want to unwrap them both like a gift to myself, and I want to weigh their cocks in both palms.

Finally, I force my shaking fingers to work, and I get them both in my hands. Jasper is slightly longer, Nate slightly thicker, and both of them make my mouth water. I slide my fists over both, drawing out matching groans, and swirl my thumbs over the tips.

"Shit. Fuck," Nate says, his head tipped back, eyes narrowed to slits.

Jasper lets out a shaky exhale. "Layla," he whispers, and buries one hand in my hair. His grip is firm but careful, and I let him guide my lips to his cock.

I press a gentle kiss to the head, then swallow him all the way down.

"Jesus Christ," Jasper grinds out, muscles rigid with restraint. His hips twitch like he wants to pound into my throat, but he cradles my head in his palm and lets me take the lead. I bob my head up and down, swirling my tongue over him as I go, breathing hard through my nose.

I pull off with a pop and lean over to spit on Nate's cock. His nostrils flare as he watches me smear the wetness over his shaft with my fist.

"I knew you were fucking dirty, Layla Maid."

I lick a stripe up his cock in answer.

I work the two of them together, jerking them both with my hands and taking turns to suck them down. Jasper is a gentleman, teeth clenching as he holds himself still, fingers playing in my hair and cradling my aching jaw.

Nate fists my hair and fucks into my throat, grunting as I hold his gaze.

I love it. I soak it all up, the gentle touches and the harsh thrusts, each ramping up my desire for the other.

When I sit back on my heels, chest heaving and chin wet, they watch me with so much longing that they look almost angry.

I slap Nate's cock against my tongue and he snaps, yanking me to my feet.

"Spread your fucking legs."

Jasper is just as wired, his touches rougher now, more possessive. The pair of them yank my shorts and panties down my legs and Nate kicks them under the hedge. Jasper crowds behind me, hooks a foot between my ankles and kicks my feet apart.

His cock prods at my naked ass, smearing wetness over my skin. His hands slide over my body, gripping and squeezing, and he tugs my top and bra down to bare my breasts.

Jasper cups them like an offering, and Nate seals his mouth on one nipple, sucking hard. The wet heat sends a pulse of sensation straight to my core, and my pussy clenches on nothing. I moan, tipping my head back on to Jasper's shoulder.

He scrapes his teeth over my neck, and I shudder. I want him to bite me, mark me, claim me. I want marks from both of them: fingertip bruises, red circles sucked on my skin.

I want my body to look like a fucking battleground.

Nate's fingers slide over my pussy, gathering the slickness. He brushes hard over my clit and I whimper, jerking in Jasper's arms.

Nate raises his head, eyes dark, and nods at Jasper behind me. Strong arms hook under my thighs and lift me up, spreading me open for Nate.

His cock nudges at my entrance before he swears and backs off again. A moment later he's back, wrapped in a condom, pushing inside. Nate reaches around me to grasp Jasper's hip, holding us all steady. I'm sealed so tight between them there's no air separating us.

My bare nipples scrape against the fabric of Nate's shirt as he starts to move. He thrusts deeper each time, forcing me against Jasper's broad chest, and his friend holds me open wide with steady hands. I can feel the throb of Nate's cock inside me, the thump of Jasper's heartbeat against my back, and I must be moaning, but I hardly notice.

I scrabble for purchase on Nate's shoulders and turn my head to lick at Jasper's jaw. He tilts his head to meet my lips, his kiss bruising, forcing my mouth wide.

It's all so much. Jasper's grip on my legs, his tongue licking into my mouth, Nate's cock sliding against my walls. My pussy starts to spasm and I let out a ragged groan, wound so tight that tears brim in my eyes.

"Come for us, Layla," Nate snarls. "Show us how you fucking come."

His thumb rubs against my clit, hard and fast, and the tension building in me snaps. I go rigid in Jasper's arms, back arched as my thighs shake. My pussy clenches down on Nate's cock, milking him as he groans and comes inside me. Jasper holds us both steady through it all, his breath hot on my neck.

My legs tremble when he sets me down, and it's a relief to drop to my knees. It only takes a few strokes before he's coming too, warm spurts hitting my bare breasts.

"Jesus," Nate says, when we've stopped gasping for breath. "Fucking Maddox doesn't know what he's missing."

Jasper hums in agreement and I lean my head against his thigh, letting my eyes fall closed for a second.

Maybe it's for the best. Taking on all four of them might kill me.

* * *

"Only one week left of summer."

Jasper rakes his fingers through my hair where my head rests on his lap. He scratches over my scalp, massaging gently.

I hum, noncommittal, and watch the trashy horror movie Nate put on in the den. It's a masterpiece of cheesy lines and red corn syrup, but that seems to be what Nate loves about it. He's sprawled on the floor, taking turns between tossing popcorn into his own mouth and at Maddox's head.

Maddox lies on another giant floor cushion, frowning at the screen. My breathing stopped when he first walked in, and the others were just as wide-eyed. But he said nothing, didn't even look in my direction. He just lowered himself down and stretched his lithe body over the cushion, like he belongs there.

Which, well, he does.

I'm the odd one out here, and Maddox and I both know it.

"Where are you living next year?" Eli asks me from the other sofa. I tense up, suspicion automatically coursing through me. Jasper must feel it, because he scratches at the sensitive skin behind my ear.

"Why?" I ask carefully.

Nate throws a look over his shoulder like I'm mad, then goes back to the movie. Maddox's eyes slide over to me, his face impassive, while Eli frowns outright.

"What do you mean, why?"

169

Anger boils up in me, and the words line up in my throat. Words about their getting me kicked out of dorms, about having no reason to trust them. But Jasper's fingers are so soft and clever in my hair, his breathing steady, and even if this is a temporary truce, I don't want to ruin it.

"It's off campus," I say shortly. "An apartment with Pierce."

Eli nods, still frowning, and goes back to the movie. A muscle tics in his jaw.

It's Maddox who speaks up, his smoky voice curling through the room.

"Why so secretive, Layla Maid?"

He turns his face to me in challenge.

Fuck it. I don't need to protect their feelings. I don't owe these guys shit.

"I don't know, maybe because last time you four knew where I lived, you got me kicked out of my dorm?"

I push off Jasper's lap to sit up. Maddox's eyes spark with triumph, and all three other boys turn to watch me warily.

"You can't think we'll turn on you again," Jasper says, almost pleading. "Everything's different this time." He reaches for my hand, but I jerk it away.

"We didn't get you kicked out last time, either." Nate tips his head to the side, the edges of his tattoo curling up his neck. His face is stony, his eyes sharp.

"Maybe not directly." Heat flushes over my cheeks, but I hold his gaze. "You told everyone to hate me, then your little minions ran me out of the dorms." I shrug bitterly. "Same difference."

Nate turns back to the film, shoulders tense. We all sit rigid, jaws locked, and only Maddox seems to be enjoying himself.

"This is a stupid fucking movie."

Nate launches to his feet. I wrap my arms around my legs and rest my chin on my knees, misery crashing through me. I *knew* there was no way we could all just move on. Fucking Maddox knew it too.

"Hold on."

Eli's command makes Nate pause halfway to the door. We all turn to him, but he's looking at me. His face is pale, but his jaw sets. I press back into the sofa cushions.

"We need to clear something up. *I* need to." Eli swallows, his eyes drifting closed for a second, and my heart shudders in my chest.

This is it. This is the part where they tear me to shreds, where they put me back in my place. I'm so fucking furious with myself for letting this happen, for trusting them for even five minutes.

But when Eli speaks again, guilt and pain drench his voice.

"Layla didn't set me up. The night of that party. I—my whole life, people have used me, manipulated me. It wouldn't have been the first or even the third time that a girl tried to blackmail me like that."

Eli breaks off, face rigid as he stares at the floor. When he finally looks up again, the tortured shame in his eyes makes my hands twitch towards him.

"I'm so sorry, Layla."

It's not me he has to worry about, though. Maddox stares at him, wide-eyed, and Nate kicks at a coffee table, swearing loudly. Even Jasper, the sweetest of the Birchwood boys, has clenched his fists at his sides.

"What the *fuck*." Nate kicks out again, destroying another piece of priceless furniture.

On the TV screen, a murderer stabs a couple having sex in a

car, red corn syrup splattering the windshield.

Maddox stands, glances at me, then strides to the bar. I know he doesn't want me anywhere near him, but tough shit. Raised voices surround me, and I slip after him, wiping my palms on my pajama pants.

His eyebrows raise when he notices me there, but I hold up a palm.

"I need a drink. That's all."

Maddox nods and puts a second glass next to his own, pouring three fingers' worth of whiskey. We drink in silence for a long moment, elbows resting on the bar.

"You've got more reason than ever to want revenge, Layla."

I hum and take another sip. "Already cashed in forty thousand dollars."

Maddox just watches me, still and deadly calm. Finally I sigh, putting my glass down with a thud.

"I wish it was a revenge thing. I'd like myself more." I spin the glass between my hands, watching amber light dance through the liquid. "At first, I thought maybe it could be that. Like I could ruin you all single-handed."

I smile, rueful. "Turns out you guys don't break easily. And turns out I'm not the ruining type. I'd love to be one of those fierce women, stomping hearts and taking names."

I look up, and he's so close my breath fans the ends of his hair. "I don't think I am, though. I'm too fucking soft."

Maddox's tongue flicks out and wets his bottom lip. "That's not a bad thing."

I shrug. I'm not so sure. My best friend got me fired less than a week ago and already I just want us back to normal.

Maddox takes my wrist and runs his thumb over my pulse point. "How do I know you won't hurt them? Ruin them like you wanted?"

He must feel the way my pulse speeds up at his touch, but I channel some of his calm.

"You don't, Maddox. That's how trust works."

I pull my wrist out of his grip and pluck my drink off the bar.

"I'll leave you to clean up." I grin and jerk my head at the mess across the room. Maddox follows my gaze, swearing softly as he takes in the state of his friends.

Not my problem. Not this time. I'm Layla Mackenzie, out to ruin movie night if not ruin lives. I swing my hips as I cross the room, and Maddox watches me go.

173

Chapter 14

The next few days at the house are surreal. Nate and Jasper are nicer to me than ever before—freakishly nice. It's like they're trying to cram a year's worth of good will into a week. They bring me coffees in the morning and drinks at night. They drag me out for walks in the gardens and drive us to beaches down the coast.

When we're alone, they make me come like their lives depend on it. I reach for them in return, but they bat my hands away and swap places, drawing orgasm after orgasm from me. They both corner me alone, too: Jasper tugs me into his bedroom and hunts me down in the pool house. Nate lays me out on the kitchen table and feasts on me at 3am.

When Maddox is near, they keep their hands to themselves—but barely. He and I settle into an easier pattern: one of politeness and personal space. I don't lean on his shoulder or play with his fingers like I do with the others, and he makes no move to touch me either.

Eli, on the other hand, suffers the brunt of his friends' wrath. All three of them are off with him, with temperatures ranging from cool—Maddox—to downright frostbitten—Nate. I'm so used to seeing him as their leader, commanding and confident, that it jars me every time I see them talk over or ignore him.

Eli rolls his eyes but takes it without complaint. I think part of him needs this. To pay some sort of price.

"I could ask them to stop," I offer one night after sneaking into his room. We're lying in his bed, sheets tangled and sweaty, my head resting on his chest.

Eli laughs, the sound rumbling through my cheek. "I'd rather you joined in."

I hate the bitter tinge to his voice. The dark shadows under his eyes when he enters the kitchen each morning. I flip over, kissing a trail down his abdomen.

"Poor baby," I croon, nipping at his hip bone. He sucks in a sharp breath, jerking beneath me. "He wants to be hated and he gets sex instead."

I slide down to his cock, hardening already, and flip my hair to one side. Eli groans, fisting my hair in one hand as I suckle on the tip.

"They should make a lifetime movie about me," he grits out. I hum and take him deep into my throat.

We're good, he and I. I'm starting to think we've been unpicking our mess for months.

"What are you going to do about Maddox?" Eli finally asks me, when we're panting and sticky from round two. He rolls off the bed and heads to the bathroom, returning with a warm, damp cloth.

He's so tender when he cleans me up, I almost can't stand it. I lie there and let him take care of me, holding my breath until it's done.

I know it's dumb. But it makes my chest hurt.

"What do you mean?" I mumble. Maddox and I are fine. We can be in the same room now, and sometimes he looks at me with something other than loathing in his eyes.

175

"He's the missing link," Eli says simply, and my heart sinks.

I know that. Eli knows that. Nate and Jasper know it too. All four of us watch Maddox with matching expressions of yearning. We practically pine after him, watching him drink his morning coffee like it's the most fascinating show we've ever watched.

Not that the guys want to get their hands on him, though it would be fucking sexy if they did.

The four of them come as a unit. They always have. I wanted to slot in, to become a fifth essential piece of the puzzle, but instead I've knocked one loose.

It's all wrong.

And Eli's right. I have to set it right.

* * *

The night is cloudless and cool, the stars bright pinpricks overhead. Maddox wasn't in his bedroom when I knocked, nor in the den with the others. When I press my face to the pool house windows, the water is glassy and still.

I'm not sure where he is, but I have an idea.

I hope I'm right. If I am, maybe he's yearning for us too.

My feet propel me over the grass, and with every step I become more sure. It's like there's a fishing line drawn between the two of us, and I can feel in my bones when he's closer.

The grove is quiet. There's only the shiver of the weeping willows, the chirrup of insects on the lake. If clouds blocked the moonlight, I might not notice him at all, but there he is, cloaked in shadows.

Maddox's back rests against a thick tree trunk. One leg stretches flat on the dirt, while his wrist rests on his other knee. He doesn't turn away from the lake when I step into the grove, but his face tightens slightly.

"Is there a problem? Do you need help with something?"

Hurt blooms in my chest, but I push it down.

"No. I came to see you."

Maddox huffs a small laugh. "To add me to your collection?"

The pain throbs harder this time, and I step back like I've been slapped. "It's not like that," I say, then for good measure: "Fuck you."

I turn and set off back the way I came. Fuck Maddox Landry and fuck what he thinks. He wants to cheapen what the rest of us have—what he could be part of if he weren't so fucking stubborn?

Fine. He can think whatever toxic crap he likes. I don't have to stand there and listen to it.

I get as far as the edge of the grove when firm hands grip my arms. Maddox spins me around and pushes me against a tree, the bark digging into my back. It's a cool night, and I'm wearing a sweatshirt and jeans, but I still grunt at the jagged edges pressing against my clothes.

Maddox doesn't ease off. He doesn't apologize and let me go, doesn't sink back into that polite indifference.

He buries his face in the hair at my neck, breathing in deep. When he straightens to stare down at me, the shadows cast over his face make him look monstrous.

"Maybe I don't want to share, Layla. Maybe I fucking wanted you first. Have you thought about that?"

His thigh slides between my legs and grinds against my core. I let out a strangled moan, gripping his shoulders. I rub against him as he flattens me to the tree, his body touching mine from our feet to our foreheads.

"I used to find you in the quad," I mumble. "I liked sitting near you."

"I know." Maddox's hands slide down my waist, his fingers spanning my whole torso. "I fucking know." His grip tightens, and I thrust against him harder, slick and wanting in my jeans. "But I never fucking did anything about it."

My breath hitches and I lunge up, catching his lip between my teeth. I bite down hard, hard enough to draw blood, then soothe it away with my tongue.

My back hits the tree when I drop back down.

"Do something now."

It's an order and a challenge. A gauntlet thrown at his feet. Maddox grips the hem of my sweatshirt and tugs it off without another word. My bra follows, then my chest is bare to the cool night air. He licks a hot stripe over one nipple then sucks the other breast into his mouth.

I groan and tug at the hem of his long-sleeved shirt, but he smacks my hands away. He flicks the button of my jeans open and slides the zipper open.

So that's how he wants it. Him dressed and in control, with me naked and vulnerable. My pussy floods, throbbing with need even as my jaw sets.

"Maybe you'd like sharing."

My voice is hoarse, but it rings through the grove. He lets go of my breast with a pop and straightens up, nostrils flaring.

"You should watch me take your friends' cocks. Maybe you'd learn something."

Maddox huffs out a sharp breath and drops to a crouch. His hands are rough as they pull my shoes and jeans off, flinging them to one side.

He doesn't pull my panties down my legs. He straightens

and curls his fingers around the flimsy lace, then tears them apart.

"Turn around." His voice is dark, and for once I don't argue. I chew on my bottom lip and face the tree, bracing both hands on the bark.

The crack of his palm on my bare ass makes me jump out of my skin. Heat blooms where he spanked me, the nerves skittering, and wetness slides down my thighs.

"You're playing with fire, Layla Maid." Maddox pushes my back down until I'm horizontal to the ground, my ass sticking out towards him. His palm smacks against my leg this time, where my ass meets my thigh.

It stings, fuck, it stings, but it makes me throb too. He smacks my bare ass again and again, rubbing the burning skin to soothe it before smacking the same spot even harder. I moan and thrust back at him, the breeze cool on my pussy.

Maddox laughs, dark and full of promise. He leans over me until his soft hair tickles my spine, until he nips at my earlobe.

"You came here spoiling for a fight, sweetheart. I'll give you one."

His sudden grip on my ass cheeks is bruising, and he spreads me apart. He moves away, the warmth of him gone from my back, then a tongue lashes up my slit.

Maddox attacks my pussy with his mouth like he's still trying to punish me. He licks me hard, setting a vicious rhythm and only breaking it to bite my thighs. I pant and squirm, gripping on to the tree as my legs shake. With each lick, I thrust back against him, burying his face in my pussy.

His thumb grazes over my clit. I whine, but he takes it away.

"No," he grumbles, resting his forehead against my ass. "I don't think you've earned that."

179

He licks me again, sliding his tongue inside, and his hand drifts over my skin. This time, though, it's the tight pucker of my ass that his thumb finds.

I cry out, pitching forwards, and it's only the firm hand on my hip that keeps me upright.

"I'm sure you know all about this," Maddox says, light and casual like this is any other conversation. He gathers the wetness of my pussy on one finger, then presses up to the first knuckle inside my ass. "What with all that sharing. You must be a pro."

"Dickhead," I gasp, my eyes screwed shut. It's sensation overload. I've thought about it dozens of times over the summer—since Jasper and Nate crowded around me at that bonfire. How it would feel to take them both inside me at once. To be that full.

None of them have pressed the issue, though.

None except Maddox.

"Tell me you don't like it."

His voice is rich, sinful. I shake my head and he laughs, pressing deeper. I nudge my hips back against him again, groaning at the slide of his finger.

"So fucking tight," he mutters, then seals his mouth to my clit. It only takes a few swirls of his tongue, then I grunt and my legs shake. The orgasm tears through me in waves, surging through my pussy and spreading all the way out to the tips of my fingers. I throw my head back with a ragged cry, the stars blurring through my tears.

"Good," Maddox says shortly, smoothing a warm palm over my lower back. He gets to his feet and I hear the rustle of his jeans, the scrape of a zipper. There's the crinkle of a foil packet too, then the broad head of his cock nudges against me.

"Where do you want me?" He asks, voice rough. "Here?" He pushes halfway into my pussy and I moan at the stretch, but he's already pulling away. He slides the tip up to my ass, and my lungs empty out. "Or here?"

"There," I croak. "But, just…"

He strokes my back again, patient while I find my words.

"Slowly."

"I'll take care of you." He plunges into my pussy again, coating his cock in my wetness. Then he starts to push against my ass, and I force myself to relax. It burns, it really fucking stings, and I almost tell him to stop.

When the head of his cock finally pushes past the ring of muscle, he rests his palm on my trembling spine.

"I'll make you feel so good, sweetheart."

True to his word, Maddox waits for me to adjust before pressing deeper. He strokes his palm over my back, making soothing sounds like I'm a skittish wild animal. It feels like it must take an age, but finally his hips meet my ass cheeks and we both sigh.

My toes curl in the dirt as my head swims. I've never been so fucking full.

"Tell me."

His voice is rough, strained, and I think distantly this must be a lot for him too.

"It's good." I lick my lips. "Really good. I… I want you to move."

It's as though my words snap the last thread of his control. Maddox thrusts against me, slow and shallow at first, his hands gripping my hips then sliding up my waist to squeeze my breasts. Heat flares in my core and I moan, thrusting back, urging him to go deeper.

181

"Fuck, Layla."

Maddox's palm smacks my ass, and I whine, tossing my hair. He's so big inside me, so huge that I can feel every inch of him. Every throb of his cock.

My pussy clenches down on nothing, but that somehow winds me even tighter. Each thrust pitches me forward, but I plant my feet and rock back, giving as good as I get.

"Are you going to come in my ass, Maddox?"

I bite my lip at the smack I knew would come. It tips me over the edge and I lurch forward, my ass pulsing around his cock. The orgasm floods through me, steady but powerful, and I let out a weak cry.

Maddox grunts and slams inside me, sealing me tight to his hips as he comes.

I'm fucking wrecked as he pulls out, sticky and sore, my legs so weak I can barely stand. Maddox uses the scraps of my ruined panties to clean me up as best he can, before helping me back into my clothes.

The house might as well be a million miles away. I collapse against the tree trunk and slide down to the ground, resting my head against the bark.

Part of me expects him to walk away. To leave and pretend this never happened.

My heart lifts when Maddox settles beside me, his side pressed against mine.

"Don't tell them you popped that particular cherry."

He snorts. "I won't if you won't."

I rest my cheek on his shoulder, the spicy scent of his shampoo filling my nose. For a moment, the summer we could have had, the *year* we could have had, taunts me. I push the thought away.

CHAPTER 14

Even if this week is all we get, it was worth it.

Chapter 15

I don't tell any of the others what happened with Maddox in the grove. I don't need to. They take one look at us at breakfast the next day, trading shy smiles and passing the butter, and they know.

I guess it doesn't hurt that we come down to breakfast together, arms brushing, Maddox's hair still damp from my shower.

"About fucking time," is all that Nate says, stabbing his cereal with a spoon.

Jasper grins at us both, even when Katerina saunters over from the kitchen and leans against the table next to him.

"Pay up, Mr Wood."

Jasper digs out his wallet and slaps a bill into her palm. She winks at me before sashaying back to the kitchen, and a flush prickles over my cheeks.

Maddox leans over to murmur in my ear, his warmth seeping over my skin. "We could have cleaned them out if we were smart about this."

"Too bad we're fucking idiots," I mutter back. "I can't believe you bet against us," I say louder, flicking a toast crumb at Jasper.

He shrugs, unrepentant. "This way it was a win-win."

Eli just looks faintly relieved.

The guys bicker and laugh together over breakfast, drawing Eli into their conversation at last after days of pointedly ignoring him. And me? I sit back in my wooden chair and soak it all in. The food is delicious: fluffy warm bread, fresh from the oven, with freshly squeezed orange juice and smoky bacon rashers. Hot scrambled eggs and a stack of steaming pancakes. The works.

Bright sunshine filters through the windows, and a breeze carries the floral scent of the gardens through the open panes.

I close my eyes and suck in a deep breath through my nose, holding it in before letting it out in a gust.

It's a perfect moment.

My mind slips to Mom and Dad in Santa Fe, so far from the sea, so far from *me*, and a pang of longing fills my chest.

Soon. One day soon I'll make the trip home; I have plenty of funds thanks to Eli's bet. And maybe I won't go alone—maybe I'll test my parents' hippie outlook with an entourage of boyfriends.

I stamp that wild hope down as soon as it blooms. This week is… everything. But I'm not an idiot. Back at college, they're the kings of campus and I'm a social outcast. And while I know they won't turn on me again, that doesn't mean they'll want to drag out this weird summer bubble.

They're four of the most gorgeous men at college. Hell, probably in the whole damn state. When they're back to crowds of female admirers, are they seriously going to turn down separate relationships just to share me?

I take a sip of lukewarm coffee, pushing my half-eaten breakfast away. I'm not hungry anymore.

"Stop frowning like we killed your fucking puppy, Layla Maid."

185

I glare at Nate, kicking his ankle under the table.

"Not your maid anymore, asshole."

"Not an asshole anymore, dick."

We grin at each other and the cold, clammy mood settling over my shoulders recedes.

Eli clears his throat and pushes back his chair at the head of the table. When he stands, their heads all swing towards him, and when he speaks, his voice rings with authority.

"Wrap this up, then let's show Layla a *real* bonfire."

I brace myself for them to snipe at him, to lash out like they've been doing since the movie night. But they all nod, swigging from coffee cups or taking a last bite of food.

He's their leader again, and it's really fucking sexy. His rich, confident voice, the set of his shoulders, his penetrating gaze. I shift in my chair and he smirks at me.

This is going to be a hell of a day.

* * *

The beach they take me to is some kind of local secret. We park in an empty dirt lot on top of a cliff: Eli, Maddox and I in the Bentley and Jasper and Nate in the sports car. The wind whips at my hair as we spill onto the lot, snatching our voices and tossing our words away.

"There," Eli yells, pointing at the edge of the cliff. I shoot him a look but trail after him as he leads us over the sparse grass.

Frothing waves crash onto the rocks below, pummeling the base of the cliff. Drops of sea water float through the air and cling to our clothes, our skin. When I lick my lips, I taste salt.

I'm about to yell in Maddox's ear, to ask if they've changed their minds about me and plan to sacrifice me to a pagan god, when Eli leads the group along the cliff side to a narrow set of steps cut directly into the rock.

"Hold tight," Maddox shouts above the wind, taking my hand and wrapping it around the rusted iron guard rail.

"Yeah, no shit," I say to the back of his head, but the wind snatches it away. And I kind of eat those words right after, because seawater soaks these steps and they're slippery as hell.

I stop after three steps and kick my flip-flops off. No way will some cheap gas station sandals be responsible for my death. With my flip-flops gripped in one hand and the other wrapped so tight around the handrail my knuckles ache, I inch my way down the cliff steps and on to the sand.

It's sheltered down here, away from the wind. The only sounds are the crashing waves and the rumbled conversation of the guys.

"Nice." I give them a shaky thumbs up. "The local death trap. Thanks for bringing me."

Eli strolls towards me, a predatory glint in his eyes. Flecks of sea foam dot his charcoal t-shirt.

"Oh, we're not there yet. There's one more hurdle."

He takes my shoulders and spins me around. Nestled on the sand against the rock face are two rowing boats. They're huge, built from thick, solid wood, with gashes marring their paint.

"Oh my God." The other three guys file past me and tip the boats right way up. Oars clatter inside them. "You really are planning a murder."

Eli squeezes my shoulders, pulling me back against his chest. "You can run any time, Layla."

He kisses a trail down my neck. My heart speeds up, my skin flushing, and I press back harder against him. He's hard in his shorts, nudging at my ass, and I grind against him.

"Lovebirds!" Nate yells, ankle-deep in the surf. "Are you coming or what?"

"Soon," Eli mutters in my ear, then he takes my wrist and tugs me to the boats. I slide in with Nate and Jasper this time, pressing my lips together when the boat rocks.

"No funny business," I tell them when Jasper climbs in at the front.

"You picked the wrong boat," Nate says behind me, then surges forwards, pushing us into the surf. When we're knee deep, he jumps in the back, the boat lurching from side to side.

"Fuck, fuck, fuck."

I curse to myself and cling to my little bench, breathing in hard through my nose. It's nothing like surfing, and queasiness coils through my belly.

I've changed my mind about the sea. This is fucking horrible.

Whatever antics Nate had in mind are a lost cause. He and Jasper row us along the coast, keeping close to the beach, and I concentrate on not throwing up on our bare feet.

I barely notice when we leave the beach behind, hugging the cliff instead. They steer the boat away from the rocks, always out past the worst waves, and point out the colonies of seabirds nesting in the cliff side.

"Awesome," I mumble, glancing up before my stomach lurches and I look back at my knees.

"Watch the horizon line."

I nod at Jasper and lick my lips, staring out across the sea. The water is blue, sparkling in the sunshine, and the horizon line is steady. As I stare at it, it's like my brain reorients, and the sickness in my gut recedes. A few minutes later, our boat nudges the sand, and Nate leaps out with a splash to push us onto shore.

I climb out with shaky legs, Jasper's hand firm on my elbow. A few feet away, Eli and Maddox drag their boat up the beach and rest it against the cliff.

The beach. Holy shit.

It's small—way smaller than the one by the house. The cliffs rise high on all sides, with no steps cut into these. The only way onto the spit of golden sand is via boat. At the back of the beach, in the middle of the sand, a pile of dried driftwood looms six feet high.

Okay, I'm back. I love the coast.

"We found it at the beginning of summer." Maddox wanders to my side as Nate and Jasper deal with our boat. "No one else comes here. It's private. Our little secret."

Dark promise curls through his voice and I shiver, all sickness gone.

We're alone, all five of us. No Katerina pushing the vacuum through the halls; no knowing looks from Diego or the gardeners.

Alone...

Holy shit.

* * *

Neither of my parents has ever seen the sea. Where I'm from, it's all desert and mountains and huge, starry skies. I love Santa Fe: I love the spicy scent of the air after a rare bout of rain, and I love the smooth adobe buildings. I love the artists everywhere, and the taste of green chili on the air whenever a cafe stews up a big vat.

I wish my Mom and Dad could see this, though. They'd be

falling over themselves, barging each other out of the way to paint it.

This beach is magic.

It's late morning by the time we arrive, and the guys each fall to their tasks like cogs in a machine. They line the giant backpacks they brought next to the boats, dipping into them as they need. Nate gathers an armful of driftwood and builds a small fire: not a grand bonfire, just big enough to sit around and breathe in the smell of wood smoke.

Jasper kneels next to him and lays out food on a blanket: a bunch of grapes, fresh baguettes wrapped in napkins, a tub of crumbly cheese, bars of chocolate, bags of chips and toffee popcorn. He lays every decent snack from the house kitchen, and digs bottles of water, juice, soda and spirits into the sand.

Maddox spreads his own supplies out in front of him and sets to work, rolling several joints.

And Eli? He takes me by the hand and pulls me towards the water. We tug our t-shirts off, dropping them on the sand. Eli's already in black swim trunks, so I wiggle my shorts down my hips and kick those off too. We stand opposite each other, taking each other in: me in a ruby-red bikini I found in a thrift store with Jasper, Eli in all his sculpted glory.

The sun soaks into my bare skin, warming my bones. I grin at the guy who, just a few weeks ago, I hated more than anyone in the world. Who bet that he could break me. Eli grabs my hand and pulls me into the water, laughing when I shriek at the cold.

It's not so bad when we swim and the blood pumps through my muscles. And it's even better when I slide my arms around his neck and wrap my legs around his waist. All that wet, bare skin pressed together, sharing warmth; the chill of his lips when I devour his mouth.

Eli groans and pulls me impossibly tighter until I feel him on every inch of me.

It's a tease. A little taste meant to drive me wild, then send me back to the beach dazed and throbbing.

They all do it, the assholes. They steal me away, one by one through the day, until I'm a trembling wreck. They kiss me with hungry mouths and hot, roaming hands, leaning against the cliff face or pressed into the sand. They kiss me like the only air they can breathe is the oxygen from my lungs, and then they tuck my hair behind my ear or spank me on the ass and send me back to the group.

Assholes.

By the time daylight fades, the sun bleeding crimson into the horizon, my entire body is a frayed nerve. Every touch, each innocent brush against my arm, makes me jump out of my skin. My pussy has been slick and aching all day, and the cool breeze wafting off the surf makes my nipples harder than granite.

They grin at each other, breaking into rumbling laughter when I shift again on the sand.

"Fuck you all," I tell them, closing my eyes and lying back on the towel Nate laid out for me. "I'll take care of this myself."

My hand smooths over my chest and down my stomach, fingertips slipping under the waistband of my bikini, before firm hands wrap around my wrists and pin them to the sand.

When I open my eyes, Maddox leans over me, his grip tight. The corner of his mouth quirks up, his eyes dancing.

"Keep her there."

Maddox nods at Eli, then rolls on top of me. Over his shoulder, I catch glimpses of the other three, tossing driftwood onto a fresh pile.

"Are you just going to do what you're told?" I goad him, rolling my hips against his thigh. "Be a good little soldier for Eli?"

Maddox shifts his leg out of reach and gives me a warning look.

"Don't be a brat."

I lunge up, licking the underside of his jaw, sucking a bruise on his neck. He sighs and shifts closer despite himself, dragging the tip of his nose through my hair.

"You always smell so fucking good."

"I've been told I taste good, too."

Maddox stops his roaming mouth and pulls back again, his grip flexing on my wrists. "Behave, sweetheart."

"Make me."

His chuckle makes me writhe.

"Don't fucking start without us," Nate yells, and I tip my head to the side.

While Maddox has been working me into a trembling mess, the others have built a driftwood bonfire and coaxed the flames to life. The fire licks along the pieces of wood, leaping towards the dim sky, flashing green in tiny bursts from the salt.

I nudge Maddox and he rolls off me, following my shaking steps to the others. Firelight dances over their faces and makes them look half wild.

My pulse thrums in my clit like a drumbeat. The waves crash and stars flicker in the dimming sky, and the heat of the bonfire creeps over my bare skin like molten lava.

I tug the strings tying my bikini undone and let it drop to the sand. They glance down with hungry eyes, then sear me with the heat of their gaze.

"Done teasing yet?" I ask in a hoarse voice. I lick my lips and someone groans.

Eli steps forward. "Oh, Layla. We're just getting started."

* * *

The last glow of daylight fades as Eli takes my shoulder and guides me down to the sand. It's firmer here, closer to the waves, and cool when I dig in my heels. My bikini bottoms are still on, but Eli makes no move to draw them down my hips.

He doesn't touch me anywhere except my wrist, capturing my arm and pinning it to the sand like Maddox did. Jasper does the same thing on my other side, and they both kneel at my head.

Nate crouches at my feet, reaching out to trace a finger over my ankle. Over his shoulder, Maddox stands with crossed arms, half his face in shadow.

I wriggle and whine, too wound up to stay still.

"Come on," I rasp, sliding my legs apart. Nate huffs and tips onto his knees between my thighs. "Stop being so fucking careful. I can take it."

"It's not about you taking it," Nate says, idly tracing up my calf and drawing a circle on the inside of my knee.

"It's about ruining you," Jasper finishes, throwing my own words back at me. I whip my head to look up at him, and the sly twist to his mouth tells me he's thinking of the same thing. The two of us, rocking and groaning together in the pool, and my promise that I'd paint him over the walls.

I grind my ass into the sand, desperate for any kind of friction. They watch me writhe and pant, pinned between them, allowing me only the feather-light touch of Nate's fingertip. He traces patterns along my thigh, my hip, then back down my stomach.

"Fucking coward," I snarl when he drifts away from my core, tracing down my other leg instead. The smile he shoots me is all sharp angles and teeth.

"Needy little maid."

If I could string a whole thought together, I'd tell all of them exactly where to go. I'd push them off and drag a boat down the beach and find my own fucking way home.

Except they've spent all day touching and teasing, coiling the need in my pussy tighter and tighter until I'm practically sobbing for them to fuck me.

It's Jasper who takes pity first. Of course it is. He hushes my whimpering and smooths a hand up my rib cage to palm my breast. He squeezes, gentler than I need, but it's still a lifeline. When Eli joins in on the other side, pinching and twisting my nipple, I arch my back and hiss out a sigh of relief.

I could come just from this, I'm so overstimulated. Joke's on them. I screw my eyes shut and reach for the orgasm hovering just out of reach, grinding my ass into the sand.

"Pull back." Maddox's voice is husky, amused. "She's going to come."

Both hands disappear from my breasts, and this time I really do let out a sob. My eyes are wet when I open them, seeking Maddox over Nate's shoulder.

"Please," I whisper just to him, throat tight. God, I need to come so badly it hurts. "Please."

Maddox smirks and steps forward, nudging Nate out of the way, and kneeling between my legs.

"Since you asked so nicely," he says, then runs a finger up my slit.

My back bows, my wrists fighting Jasper and Eli's grip, and I lift my hips to chase his touch. It's slow, teasing, but he doesn't pull away, twisting his hand to slide two fingers inside me. He curls them, stroking a spot on my inner walls, relief shuddering through my core, and then I'm coming on his hand. My legs lock together, holding him in place, and waves of tremors wrack through me, one after the other.

Finally, I slump back, blinking bleary eyes. I go to push my hair out of my face, but Jasper holds my wrist firm.

The inferno in my core roars back to life, and I understand now why they've teased me all day. That orgasm, despite the way it tore through me, barely took the edge off. Already, I'm panting and needy again, wetness sliding between my thighs.

The want they've stoked inside me is a black hole, feeding and feeding on every touch, every sensation, and never satisfied.

They could fuck me all night without stopping, and it wouldn't be enough. The shower of condom packets on the sand next to me says Nate has had the same thought. He crouches next to me, running a palm over my trembling stomach.

"Just thinking ahead." He flashes those teeth at me again. "I won't be done with you until morning."

I nod, arching my stomach into his touch. He growls, hooking his fingers in my bikini bottoms and tugging them roughly down my thighs. Maddox takes over when they reach my knees, pulling my legs up in the air to drag the scrap of fabric over my ankles.

He lets go of my legs, but I don't lower them back to the sand. I spread them and rest them on his shoulders, earning another chuckle. Nate tosses him a condom and he pushes his shorts down his hips, pulling his hard cock out.

They all look so fucking good in the firelight. Every inch of bare skin is tinted gold, glowing and warm.

"Greedy girl," Maddox mutters, then he pushes inside. He's not tentative like last night, waiting for me to adjust: he slides firmly into my slick pussy, stretching me with a harsh sigh.

"Have you told them what you did for me by the lake, baby?"

His hips move in short pumps. I shake my head, not really listening, thrusting my hips up to take him deeper.

"What are you talking about?" Eli asks, but Maddox ignores him.

"Maybe we shouldn't tell them." He squeezes my hip, then trails a finger through the wetness of my pussy. When he reaches down and slides a fingertip into my ass, I groan and the others let out a string of curses. "Maybe we should show them instead."

Nate tosses a bottle of lube at Maddox like he hopes it'll take his fucking head off. "If you're going to do it, do it properly," he bites out.

Maddox catches it easily and hums. "Layla's plenty wet, aren't you, sweetheart?"

But he snaps the bottle open anyway, slowing his hips while he coats his fingers. They feel so good rubbing my ass I start babbling at the sky.

"Yes. Fuck. I want that. I want to show them everything."

For someone who supposedly didn't want to share me, Maddox is pretty fucking generous. He jerks his head at Nate, calling him closer, and pulls out to flip me onto my stomach. As soon as I'm turned over, Eli and Jasper fasten onto my wrists again.

It's maddening, not being able to see what they're doing.

I can feel the two of them moving behind me, positioning themselves between my splayed thighs, and I can feel the warmth of the bonfire licking over my bare skin.

I rest my cheek on the sand and try to take deep, slow breaths. To settle myself. Jasper's thumb traces the inside of my wrist, and I smile up at him.

"Look at you." He leans down to murmur in my ear, his words just for us. "Spread out for us in the firelight. I could swallow you whole."

"*Yes*," I hiss, as Nate pushes inside me. I don't need to look back; I know each of them by heart, their specific touch seared into my soul. "Do it."

Maddox's fingers are next: one first, in my ass, then a second swiftly after. He works me with purpose, sliding in and out, stretching my hole. The burn of his fingers and the sharp snap of Nate's hips make my eyes roll back in my head. They fuck me together, a perfect rhythm, until I'm a sweating, shaking mess.

"Fuck." I grind my forehead into the sand, my pinned hands scrabbling. By some unspoken communication, Nate's hips slow and he pulls out, reluctance clear in every tortuously slow inch. Eli lets go of my wrist and after a moment's absence, he lies on his back at my side.

"Come here, Layla."

I push myself onto wobbly arms and knees, Jasper releasing my wrist. Eli's already naked, a condom rolled onto the hard cock jutting away from his stomach. My limbs tremble and jerk as I crawl over to him, a puppet with snipped, tangled strings.

It doesn't help that Maddox stays with me, his fingers curled deep in my ass.

"Good girl." Eli lets out a harsh breath as I sink down onto him in one movement. Maddox allows me three messy rolls of my hips before he draws his fingers out and nudges my ass with his cock.

It's so much. Almost too much. Too much stretch, too much sensation. The muscles in my back twitch and shiver under Maddox's soothing palm. He goes slow, steady but insistent, and Eli lays like a statue underneath me. Both of them waiting for the burn to subside and for my lungs to work again.

They don't have to wait long. The ringing in my ears fades away, and the hush of the waves takes its place. All four of the guys are breathing hard, Eli's chest rising and plummeting beneath my hot cheek.

"Stay with me, Layla." His fingers card through my hair, trace along my jaw. I struggle up onto my palms, pressing my lips desperately to his. Eli groans and kisses me back, the hum reverberating through his chest, and the need in my pussy roars into an inferno. I throw my hips back, grinding against him, and Maddox grips me and sets us a rhythm.

I keep kissing Eli, messy and open-mouthed, until a hand snakes around my throat and jerks me upright. I slam back into Maddox's chest, his arms caging me in as he fucks me hard.

"Don't forget the rest of us, sweetheart."

His words are soft, but his teeth on my neck are rough. Maddox twists my face to his, thrusting his tongue inside my mouth like he wants to lick away all trace of Eli. I cling to his forearm, suckling on his tongue, lips quirking at the approving smack on my ass.

My back is bowed, my spine screaming, and I gasp with relief when he drops me back to Eli's chest.

It's like that for hours. The four of them, by turns moving in sync and battling for dominance. Eli and Maddox are the worst for it, Eli commanding me with a murmur and Maddox with a snarl. But Nate gets pushy too, when he's been on the sidelines too long—shouldering the others out of the way and snapping if they resist.

Jasper's the happiest to hold back, but not because he's timid. He watches me the most intently, a possessive worship on his face, and when he pushes inside me, he rolls on top, keeping the others away.

"They can scrap over you like hyenas if they want."

He brushes the hair from my eyes and kisses my temple, the corner of my mouth. He's gentle with me, mindful of my poor, battered pussy. The way his hips swirl against mine reminds me of his dancing: sensual, elegant, crackling with coiled strength.

"I'll wait them out and have you all to myself."

The orgasm he coaxes from me is slower to build than the rest, but when it breaks over me it floods through my whole body, wracking my frame. Jasper lets go and we cling together, coming as one.

After, he kisses the tears from the corner of my eyes.

"Such a weeper, Layla. I love it."

We fuck until the bonfire burns down to ashes and the sky pales before dawn. And when we collapse together in a sweaty, sandy tangle, my body is sore but my heart sings.

I'll remember this night for the rest of my life. These four are written in my body now, their signatures carved on my soul. Whatever happens after this week—no matter the bittersweet goodbyes—no one can take this night from me.

Darkness claims me, and I go with a smile.

Chapter 16

"Layla Mackenzie, I swear to God, get your ass out that door."

Pierce shoos me away from the living room window in our new apartment, where I've been staring at the street in a daze. The trees that line the sidewalks are already turning red and gold, their leaves crisping on the branch.

"Sorry, yeah."

I sling my backpack over my shoulder, brushing a dust mark off my old jeans. The first day of a new semester never feels real: I drift through my classes, collecting class schedules and trying not to get overwhelmed by the looming workload.

Last year, I dreaded every moment spent on campus. I ducked into empty classrooms and janitors' cupboards whenever people started whispering about me.

This year, my former tormentors have each messaged me already this morning. Eli offered to drive us to campus; Jasper suggested grabbing coffee before class.

I ignored them all. I'm not angry anymore, not after everything that's happened, but the memories of how miserable they once made me are stronger now we're back at college. I don't want the first day of another semester to be dominated by the Birchwood boys.

I don't need them—not for this. Not to claim my rightful space at college. And I don't want a front row seat when they're reunited with their admirers; when they remember how many dozens of other girls would kill to date any one of them.

We live closer to campus this year. Close enough to walk when the weather's good. Pierce and I fall into step, her happy chatter washing over me.

She was pretty fucking relieved that I still wanted to live with her. And sure, it would have been a nightmare to try and find somewhere else short notice.

That's not why I forgave her, though. Pierce fucked up—no way around it—but one thing I know for sure. She has always wanted good things for me. She stuck by me, protected me when no one else did.

There's no one else I want to start this semester with.

"Are we expecting company any time today?"

Pierce's tone is polite, careful. I know full well that she thinks I'm an idiot for letting any one of those guys near, let alone all four. And she's watched up close as the tension ratcheted tighter in me over the last week as the new semester approached.

She's worried that they'll hurt me.

I'm scared that she's right. But not for the reason she thinks.

I know in my soul that the Birchwood boys won't give me any trouble, today or any other day. But it's not their anger I'm worried about.

It's their indifference.

"Not sure." I shrug, and thankfully Pierce takes the hint and changes the subject. She works herself up into a rant about library hours, and I nod and agree in all the right places. Even when we cross into campus and my heart starts to pound, I force myself to play along.

"You don't have to do this, you know."

"Huh?"

"Pretend everything's fine."

Pierce fixes me with a knowing look, and I wipe my damp palms on my jeans. The truth is, I haven't been fine since the day we left the coast. I miss the guys like a phantom limb, their absence painful and prickling. I catch myself talking to Jasper in my head, or wanting to show Nate dumb stuff on my phone. I reach for Eli when I roll over at night and touch myself imagining Maddox's hands.

They've tried to call me dozens of times in the week we've been apart. They've texted suggesting movie nights, dinners, straight up orgies.

I haven't replied to any of them. I can't bear to see the way they look at me change. And it must change, now that we're out of our summer bubble. Now that we're back to reality.

It's not like sharing is their thing. Something they've done before; that all of them are into. They shared me because they all wanted me, and because I was right there, and it was temporary. For them, this summer was a wild experiment—something to look back on for a remembered thrill.

It was so much more for me. That's why I can't just be friends.

"Let's just get through this day, then find some cheap-ass cocktails."

Pierce laughs. "Amen."

* * *

In the end, we don't get through the day. We barely reach the afternoon. I sit with Pierce in the quad, sprawled on the grass while the heat from summer holds on. I've just taken a fucking huge mouthful of falafel when Nate throws himself down at my side.

"What the fuck, Layla Maid."

I choke on my wrap, spraying lettuce everywhere. Nate glares while I force myself to swallow and suck down a few breaths. Pierce glances between us and scoops up her bag, quietly drifting away.

"I am so fucking angry with you."

I believe him. Nate's hasn't looked at me this coldly for weeks. I swallow a gulp of soda and wipe my sleeve over my streaming cheeks.

"I'm sorry," I croak, because Nate has bags under his eyes. His mouth is turned down, his lips pressed tight, and I hate that I'm the one who made him look so drawn.

Nate crosses his arms, unimpressed. "You want to tell me what the fuck's going on? Finish with us if you must, Mackenzie, but have the guts to do it right. I never thought you of all people would be such a fucking coward."

I shake my head, but what can I say, really? He's right. I got scared, and I ran.

"I'm sorry," I say again, and Nate sighs, disappointed.

I don't blame him. I'm disappointed in myself too.

"I really do want to be friends," I start, forcing myself to grow the fuck up. Nate rears back, something flashing through his eyes, but I force myself to carry on. He deserves an explanation. "It's just hard at the moment. So soon after the summer. After everything that happened. I know it was just fun, a summer fling and all that, but I've never been good at casual. At not getting hurt."

Nate blinks, shaking his head like he's trying to knock things into place.

"What the fuck are you talking about?"

I sigh, irritated now too. "I just need some fucking space, all right? Some time to… process. Move on. We can hang out once my head's on straight."

Nate inhales sharply and digs his phone out of his pocket, stabbing at the screen.

"For a smart girl, you're fucking dense, you know that?"

He stands and grabs my elbow, pulling me up with him. I barely have time to snatch my backpack before he's frog-marching me across the quad.

A warm suspicion curls through my stomach, but I push it down. I won't hope. Not yet.

"Eat your fucking lunch," Nate mutters as we walk, but I toss my wrap in the trash as we pass. Not to wind him up, though a thrill zips up my spine when he bristles.

I'm not hungry. My stomach, my chest, my entire damn body is churning. With nerves, and with something else.

Anticipation.

Nate leads me to an empty lecture hall, planting me on the lecturer's desk. Sunshine spills through the windows in broad shafts, dust motes spinning in the light.

"Are you going to teach me a lesson?"

I smirk at the angry boy with his tattoos and his hard eyes. He huffs and throws his backpack onto the floor, the sound echoing through the room.

He can't hide his slight smile, though. He knows what's going on. So do I. I may sometimes be fucking dense, like Nate says, but I'm finally starting to get it.

When Eli, Jasper and Maddox slip into the lecture hall, closing the door with a snap, I know two things for sure: I'm the world's biggest idiot, and I haven't breathed right since they've been gone.

"Layla here thinks we're all fucking around." Nate leans against the first row of desks, his arms crossed. "That's why she decided to fucking ghost us."

The other three boys whip around to stare at me. I glare at Nate.

"That's *not* what I said."

I expect Eli or Maddox to saunter forwards, to clip out a demand. But it's Jasper who steps up onto the platform, his hands shoved in his pockets. His casual outfits from the summer are gone; his dark pants and tailored shirts are back.

"Then what did you say?"

The last week has not been kind to Jasper. Even though his clothes are pressed and perfect, his face is pale and his wavy blond hair is rumpled. It's not just him, either—they all look as miserable and exhausted as I feel.

God, I'm an ass.

"I… I didn't want to see you all go back to normal. Here, you've all got girls tripping over themselves to date you. And I know none of you wanted to share me, not really. It wouldn't be fair of me to ask that, to date all four of you and demand you only date me. Because that's what I'd want."

I raise my chin and stare them each in the eye. This will be my only chance to say it.

"I want all four of you, and I want you all to myself. And I don't just want fucking, I want the rest too. Heart and soul. So unless you can offer me that, you need to give me some space."

Jasper glances over at Maddox and Eli. Nate just stares at

me.

"I *am* sorry for ghosting," I tag on lamely, hands gripping the desk. "I guess I should have said all this sooner."

Nate scoffs. "No fucking shit."

But he grins at me as he says it. And Jasper, he strides straight over to me, clutching me to his chest like it's been years, not seven days.

"We'll find a way for you to make it up to us." Maddox's smoky voice curls over my shoulder. Eli's fingers play with my hair on my other side, and I sigh, melting into Jasper's chest.

This is happening. It's real.

Fucking hell.

* * *

Pierce whistles when I find her before the next class, all four guys in tow. Jasper grips my hand, not bothered by my damp palm, and Eli walks so close on my other side that our forearms brush together.

"Well, you'll certainly make a statement."

Her eyes flick between us, a slight frown creasing her forehead.

She'll come around. She's been protecting me from them for so long, it's her instinct to want them gone. But she'll soon see the way they look at me. The way they form a barrier around me in crowds; the way they jostle for space by my side.

"It's not a fucking statement," Nate snaps. "Who gives a shit what these idiots think?"

I roll my eyes and tune out their bickering, gazing around the quad.

Campus is filling up by the hour, herds of new and veteran

students moving between builds and breaking away to sprawl on the grass. Everywhere I look are brand new backpacks and stacks of shiny textbooks. The delicious scent of garlic and spices floats on the breeze from the food trucks, and a coffee seller on a bicycle trundles his way through the crowds, ringing his bell.

This year will be better. The trees shiver, and goosebumps ripple up my arms. I lean into Eli's shoulder, so warm and sculpted through the fabric of our shirts, and he winks down at me.

"Are you ready to make waves, Layla Mackenzie?"

Yeah. I think I am.

Author's Note

Thank you for reading Lords of Summer! As my debut novel, it was truly nerve-wracking to fling it into the ether. I hope you enjoyed reading it as much as I loved writing it.

Well. On the good days, anyway.

Since you DID read it, I would be super grateful if you took the time to rate and review! Reviews really help readers and authors to find each other—plus you can check off your good deed for the day :)

Read on for some sneaky bonus content, plus a teaser from the next book in the *Year of the Harem* collection: *Autumn Tricksters*.

The Year of the Harem is just beginning…

Let's keep in touch!

If you enjoy my work and want to be the first to know what I'm up to, please consider **signing up for my newsletter!** I send bonus content, amazing book recommendations, cover reveals, and other goodies twice a month.

Subscribers get a free download of my *Lords of Summer* prequel: *Before the Fall.* This short story follows the events of that fated party… from Maddox's eyes.

Here's a sneak peek…

* * *

She's here.

She's arrived in the quad.

Layla Mackenzie.

I glance up between the curtain of my dark hair, my elbows resting on my knees. It's still early September, barely the start of second year, and summer hasn't relinquished its hold. The air is warm—warm enough that the students dotted around the grass and on the benches are still in t-shirts. They kick back, legs stretched out, laughing in groups or studying solo.

It's the beginning of the year, and everything feels heavy

with promise. With potential.

Layla picks her way across the grass, stepping over out-stretched legs and winding between abandoned backpacks. She nods at a few of the groups; waves at a couple of solo students. They wave back, calling out her name, inviting her to join them.

Everyone loves Layla. What's not to love? The buttery sunshine dances over her, drawing deep bronze highlights out of her dark red hair.

Fuck.

No one makes an ass of me like Layla. I look at her creamy skin, her sweet, cheeky smile, and all words dry up in my throat. The only thing that hurts worse than looking at her is not looking at her, and every second in her presence is a sweet torture. And all the while that I'm here dying, she has no clue. She probably doesn't even know my name.

It doesn't matter. She's too good, too happy for me to let myself get near. I'm not built for sweet girls, nor for holding hands on the way to class. No gentle kisses in the sunshine. No: if I got my calloused hands on her, she'd come away stained.

I couldn't bear that.

As if she can hear my thoughts, Layla glances in the direction of my bench, and I drop my gaze to my hands. I run a thumb over the opposite knuckle, back and forth, feigning interest in the scars flecking my skin.

It was a rough summer back home. It always is. Rough, but satisfying: endless days of back-breaking labor, sweetened by the jokes between workers, and at the end of the season, the tangible results. Our family ranch was built on sweat and blood, started from the ground up. It's bigger now, one of the most successful in the state, but the demands are bigger too.

The blood and sweat never go away; it's a yearly tithe, and we pay it.

I risk a glance at Layla again, to see which lucky bastards she decided to sit with, but she's gone from the center of the quad. My head jerks up fully, and I whip my gaze around, only to find her sat a few feet away on the next bench over.

My heart speeds in my chest, hammering against my rib cage, and my mouth goes dry.

Fuck. This is the problem: this is what she does to me.

She makes me foolish, reckless. Raw.

Layla sees me looking around like I've lost my puppy, because of course she does - she's not blind. I lose sight of her for fifteen seconds and the panic practically bleeds from my pores. She's not the only one who notices either; the nearest group lazing on the grass are watching me curiously too.

I let my eyes meet hers for a split second, then slide my gaze away, like I'm still looking. Like I haven't found who I'm searching for.

I swear she deflates just a little.

Fuck. I want to go over there, to just snatch up my stuff and march over to sit beside her. I want to snuff out any doubt in her mind that she's the one I'm looking for—she's always the one.

Every day, I come to the quad during lunch for the sole purpose of seeing her. I sit on this bench, or lay out on the grass—that part isn't important. What's important is that she always comes too, usually alone. And she always seems to pick out a spot near me to sit.

I don't kid myself that she does it on purpose. We've barely said ten words to each other, even since Eli started bringing her to hang out with our group. But maybe—subconsciously—she's as drawn to me as I am to her. Maybe she feels the same pull, the same fishing hook in her gut tugging her towards me.

The only relief is when she's near. Then I can breathe again.

God, I sound fucking insane.

See, this is why I can't bother the girl. If I say any of this shit out loud, if I tell her how she makes me feel, I'll be locked away in a padded room and they'll be right to do it.

Better to enjoy these stolen moments with her, then force myself back to my day.

It's not like I can tell the others, either. Eli, Jasper and Nate. I've seen the way they look at her too. We're all as fucking bad as each other.

Jealousy curls through me, hot and vicious, whenever any of my friends talk to her. And though they've never acknowledged it, they seek her out almost as much as I do. At least once a week, I'll see Jasper stood behind her in line at the campus coffee shop, leaning down with a smile curling his lips to murmur in her ear. His wavy blond hair slides forward, tickling at her cheek.

I see the shiver that runs up her spine, too. It makes me want to tear him away from her, to throw him through the huge glass window.

But when he catches up with me a few minutes later, coffee in hand, I always force a smile. What am I going to say, anyway? Hey, man, that's my dream woman that I never plan to speak to?

Nate and Eli are just as bad. Nate gets this feral glint in his eye whenever she's near, like he's putting out pheromones or some shit. A lot of girls are scared of Nate, with his buzzed head and the tattoos all over his arms and chest. But he makes

Layla laugh with his savage words, the sound ringing bright between the pale stone buildings.

I long for the sound of her laugh even as I hate that I'm not the one to draw it from her.

Eli is the worst of all. He spoke to her first, got to know her in some tutorial group, so he thinks he has some kind of claim on her. It makes me want to fucking scream when he tucks an arm around her shoulders, possessive and sure.

I saw her first. I fucking craved her first.

I just never did anything about it.

Eli and Jasper round the corner to the quad, moving with confident strides. They laugh and talk as they walk, raising a hand each when they notice me. We found each other during orientation week of first year, Nate included. It was so fucking easy, like four jigsaw pieces slotting into place.

I've never had that before. Not with friends, and certainly not with family. What we have, the four of us—it's like breathing. Unconscious and vital.

Both of their eyes light up when they notice Layla on the next bench over. I have to remind myself then that these guys are brothers to me —that I can't lose my shit over a dumb surge of jealousy.

Then Eli strides straight past my bench to sit next to Layla. A dark curl falls over his forehead, and his eyes crinkle when he speaks.

No. No, he can't tuck her hair behind her ear—can't make her blush like that. I shoot a glance at Jasper to see what he thinks, but he's watching the two of them with heat in his gaze. I want to shake him, then rip Eli away from Layla and shake him too. Can't they see how wrong this is?

It should be me on that fucking bench.

I tried to stay away for so long. Since the first time I saw Layla, way back in October of first year. I thought I could protect us both by keeping away, but now she's everywhere I look, and my friends have set their sights on her.

Fuck that. I won't bow out without a fight.

Today is the day I tell Layla Mackenzie how I feel.

* * *

"I'm going to ask her out."

Eli frowns at me, confused. "Who?"

Have I really been that fucking inscrutable? Whenever I'm near Layla, I feel like there's a glowing neon sign on my forehead that says 'PSYCHO WITH A CRUSH.'

I guess I've been better at playing it cool than I realized. Of course, that's only going to make this conversation more awkward.

I glance at my friend—my brother. The guy who became a part of me almost as soon as we met. He's sprawled in the chair next to me in the back row of the lecture hall. We all got in the habit of sitting in the back last year, as soon as we found out Nate is far sighted. He's not even in this class with us, but we still strode to the back row on autopilot.

Eli comes from a political family, and he has that Kennedy vibe going on. He's handsome and clean cut, with a face for fundraisers and garden parties, but with a dangerous edge to him. Girls fucking love him, and I guess Layla is no exception.

No. I can't just walk away without even trying. Even if it does piss Eli off.

I look him in the eye when I say it.

"Layla Mackenzie. I'm going to ask her out."

I expect him to be pissed, but I don't expect the hurt and panic that flash through his eyes.

"Layla? What the fuck, Maddox? What are you trying to pull?"

I shrug, hating the way he's gone rigid in his chair, but not willing to take it back. There's too much at stake here, and it's better he hears it now before anything more has happened between them.

"I like her too. I have for a while. I'm going to ask her out."

Eli's nostrils flare and he turns his head, staring down at the lecturer prepping his slides. He mutters something under his breath, something like "All fucking three of you..."

I don't shift in my chair. I don't fiddle with my pen. I'm not the nervous type—at least when I'm far from Layla. And though unease curls in my gut as the silence stretches on and the lecture begins without Eli speaking again, I focus. I take notes and watch the slides, only half aware of the tension between us.

Eli waits until the lecture has ended and the other students are packing up before he speaks. He turns to me again, jaw tense, the rumble of conversation and footsteps covering his words.

"I'm not going to step aside, Maddox. You don't have a damn claim."

I nod, even though I know in my bones that's not true.

"I don't expect you to."

Eli jerks his chin down, and then he's up, swinging his backpack onto his shoulder. I follow, gathering my things with sure, steady hands.

As Eli walks down the steps in front of me, his shoulders are rigid under his shirt. I wish I could slap a hand on his back, tell him I'm fucking with him and this is my idea of a really shit joke, but I can't. My words have put something in motion that can't be stopped. All I can do now is go forward, and hope I still have Eli at the end of this mess.

We usually grab coffee together after this class, but Eli strides away without a word. I don't follow. He clearly needs a minute, and he's not the only one. I tip my head back and breathe a lungful of air.

Eli's right. What am I doing? What happened to Layla being too good for me? Have I really just fucked up one of the most important relationships in my life, just because I got jealous?

"Hey, man."

Nate's hand smacks hard against my shoulder. Everything about Nate Becker is hard: his words, his smile, his movements. It's part of why we get on so well: no bullshit. No tip toeing around. Only sharp jokes and gruff words and tough love.

"You've got some fucking explaining to do."

Nate hooks his thumbs in his pockets, a smile showing his teeth.

"Eli tell you already?" I grunt.

"The second you tossed that little grenade."

I sigh. "I shouldn't have fucking said anything."

Nate shakes his head, smile growing. "No way, man. This is exactly what we need. I'm glad you fucking said it, or I'd have to."

Sometimes, it's like Nate and I share brain waves. We know what each other is thinking without even looking over.

And other times, it's like this, and he speaks in fucking tongues.

"I don't follow."

Nate spreads his arms, savage grin tilted at the sky.

"Battle royale, man. Four v. four. For our lovely Layla Mackenzie."

No. I never expected Eli to step aside without a fight, but this is the last thing I need. I've seen Jasper and Nate with Layla—they've both got as good a shot with her as any of us. The thought of them both making a play for her —flirting, touching her—I blink away the red haze that clouds my eyes.

I guess this is how Eli just felt.

He was pretty fucking dignified, all things considered.

Me, I want to roar at Nate and tackle him to the ground. I want to hunt down Jasper between his classes and put the fear of God in him.

I don't, because I'm not a fucking animal, and because they all deserve better than that shit. Layla included.

But I still want to. The urge snakes through me and settles in my chest.

"Battle royale." I nod at Nate. "It's on."

Teaser: Autumn Tricksters

The circus can be deadly. It's smoke and mirrors; misfits and flames.

It's the place where tricksters come to play.

They sent me away with a broken wrist and a broken heart.
  Now I'm back, with fire burning in my veins.

I live for the pounding drumbeats, for the savagery and applause.
  The circus calls to my soul; three men in particular.

The ringmaster, the acrobat, and the fire-eater.
  My boss, my ex's brother, and the thief in the shadows.

I don't trust them for a second, but I'll play their wicked games.

Autumn Tricksters is the second book in the Year of the Harem series. It is a standalone reverse harem novel and contains explicit language, steamy sex and m/m content.

Release date: October 2nd 2020.

Read on for a sneak preview…

* * *

I step one foot back in the carnival and thank god I'm home. Three weeks in Ohio with my straight-laced family was a nightmare. I haven't breathed right since I left this place, since I heard the shriek of the crowd, the roar of flames, the pounding of drums. The scent of popcorn and roasting nuts floats to me on the breeze, and my stomach rumbles.

Finally. It's been three weeks too long.

I nod to the men and women running the stalls. There are shooting games, with the *plink* of air rifle pellets and the clatter of cans dropping to the ground. There are drinks stalls, with fresh roasting coffee and beer on tap. There are tents with fortune tellers; mimes with painted faces, striding through the crowd on stilts; pink vats of cotton candy.

It's a wonderland. An eerie, feral wonderland, where you're just as likely to have your pocket picked as your fortune told.

No sticky fingers come near my pockets. I'm one of these people, and they know better than to go for their own.

I hitch my duffel bag up on my shoulder and weave my way across the carnival grounds. The drink is flowing tonight; the townies getting messy and loud. They shove each other and cackle, their inhibitions slipping away in the carnival's haze. I skip around them, no one coming within an inch of my skin.

Sure, I could stamp my steel-toed boots and barge my way through. But I've had an eight-hour journey with a caffeine headache and a throbbing wrist. I know when to pick my battles. So I duck and weave my way through the crowd, like they're rocks and I'm water flowing around them.

"Hazel!" An older woman running one of the food stands yells and waves her entire arm. I grin and cut over to her,

219

sniffing at the hot dogs grilling on her cart.

"Hey, Ginny."

I drop my duffel at the base of her stand. Two soft, plump arms wrap around me and pull me close, and I pat her back awkwardly with my cast. When I pull away, one of her long gray hairs sticks to my tongue. I spit it out, grimacing at her roar of laughter.

"You've been away too long, girl."

"Tell me about it."

If I'd had my way, I'd never have left at all. Not even after everything that happened. This is my home.

"Robbie gave you the green light to come back?"

I shrug. "Something like that."

Ginny slices a bun as she talks, her hand deft with the knife. Ginny may look like a sweet old grandma, with her salt and pepper hair and flowery smock dresses, but she can gut a troublemaker quicker than a fish.

The truth is, I never asked for permission to come back. I should never have let them send me away at all. If I hadn't been so messed up—freaking out over my busted wrist, heart cracked open by my asshole ex—I'd have stood my ground. Insisted on staying here and resting up in my trailer.

Being home did nothing for me. I didn't get to laze around and eat my Mama's treats, or whatever Robbie expected. I got lectures and disappointed sighs. Pointed looks at my tattoos, my inky purple hair. Raised blood pressure and my fill of fucking cornfields.

Yeah. That was no healing retreat. If Robbie wants to send me away to lick my wounds, next time he can shell out for a spa.

Ginny pushes a steaming hot dog into my unbroken hand,

loaded up with fried onions. I groan and snatch up the mustard and ketchup, lashing them on top.

"You're a goddess. A fucking deity." I take a bite and my eyes practically cross.

Ginny laughs and slaps me hard on the back, hard enough that I lose some onions.

"Get gone before Robbie sees you. I ain't wading into that."

It's more than fair, so I balance my hot dog on my cast and swing my duffel back onto my shoulder. Robbie will ream me out when he sees I'm here, and there's no call to drag Ginny into that. Robbie may be young, may be quiet and watchful, but he runs this entire show. When he says jump, we ask how high.

Apart from me, I guess. Just this one time.

I take another bite of my hot dog, burning the roof of my mouth, and plunge back into the mass of people. It's dark, the air nipped with autumn cold, and the flames of the fire eaters burst in glowing pillars over the heads of the crowd. I take one look at those flames and change course.

I'm not in the mood for Kamran Lajani.

Pounding drums sound from the big top tent on the edge of the carnival. I stare at it for a moment, almost sick with longing. I should be in there right now; I should be on that trapeze. Soaring weightless over the crowd, twisting and swinging, buoyed by their gasps. Chalk coating my palms and crammed under my nails. Sweat slicking my skin.

I grunt and tuck my cast to my chest, shoving the last of my hot dog in my mouth.

Soon. Then I'll show these fuckers what's up.

I hate to go in there when I can't perform, but I head for white hulking mass of that tent. Robbie keeps a watchful eye over the whole of the carnival, but he's especially careful with the circus acts. The performers put their lives on the line with every single performance. Even with safety nets and hidden lines, there are some risks you just can't mitigate.

Robbie fucking hates that. When Yan dropped me three weeks ago—dropped me in all the possible ways—I became a prime example of the risks of aerial work.

He won't be happy to see me back so soon. Well, tough shit.

I duck through a slit in the canvas at the side of the tent, away from the bustling entrance. My duffel catches on the flap and I instinctively flex my hand in my cast, hissing at the burning hot lash of pain. Wrenching myself free, I blink away the tears brimming in my eyes.

Fucking tent.

Robbie is exactly where I thought he'd be. He stands with his boots planted and his arms crossed, eyes glued on the performer spinning overhead. I glance up, following his line of sight—it's Aleksi, our star performer. I used to love watching him work, watching the fluid way he spun on the silks like a spider weaving a web.

But Aleksi is the spitting image of his brother Yan, and the sight of him now makes my hot dog lurch in my stomach.

Doesn't matter. I duck my head and make a beeline for the man in charge. If any visitors were to glance at Robbie, they'd probably think he was a roadie. He's young, early thirties with sandy blond hair and scruff on his chin. He dresses all in faded black: thick work pants and a long-sleeved t-shirt. A tool belt is slung around his hips, and a radio crackles on the belt.

First rule of the carnival: appearances can be deceiving. He's not just some roadie. Robbie's our puppet master.

"Hey, boss." I give him my most winning smile as I plant

222

myself square in front of him. Better not to dance around the point—I came back uninvited.

Robbie's eyes flick down, and irritation ripples across his face. He lowers his chin to stare me down, jaw clenching.

"Did I say you could come back?"

His Scottish accent always makes him sound softer than he really is.

"Probably not," I say cheerfully, dropping my duffel at his feet. "But I got this sixth sense. Figured you missed me."

"You figured wrong." Robbie nudges my bag with his boot, nose wrinkling like I've brought him a dead mouse. "You messed yourself up. You can't work like that, Hazel."

He means my busted wrist. The bones still throb in my cast. I know he's right, that there's no reason for him to house and feed me while I can't even perform, but there is no way on this planet I'm about to turn tail and slink back off to the cornfields.

"I'll work a stand. Hook-a-Duck or some shit." I force another smile, trying not to let the hurt reach my face. I know Robbie's my boss and he doesn't owe me shit, but it's cold for him to dismiss me like that. Like I hurt myself because I was careless, not like a cheating scumbag literally dropped me.

Like this isn't my home just as much as his.

Come on, man, I urge him in my brain. Muster up an emotion.

Robbie looks at me, face as blank as a marble statue, then slides his gaze back up to Aleksi.

"Fine," he mutters, not even looking at me anymore. "But you'll earn your keep, same as everyone else."

Asshole. I never said I wouldn't, and I resent the implication. But I keep my face carefully blank to match his, leaning down to scoop up my duffel.

223

"Always a pleasure, boss man."
Robbie rolls his eyes without even looking down.

About the Author

Kayla Wren is a British author who writes steamy New Adult romance. She loves Reverse Harem, Enemies-to-Lovers, and Forbidden Love tropes.

Kayla writes prickly men with hearts of gold, secretly-sexy geeks, and—best of all—she's ALWAYS had a thing for the villains.

You can connect with me on:
- 🌐 https://www.kaylawrenauthor.com
- 📘 https://www.facebook.com/kaylawrenauthor
- 🔗 https://www.bookbub.com/authors/kayla-wren
- 🔗 https://www.amazon.com/author/kaylawren

Subscribe to my newsletter:
- ✉ https://newsletter.kaylawrenauthor.com/beforethefall

Also by Kayla Wren

Autumn Tricksters
The circus can be deadly. It's smoke and mirrors; misfits and flames.

It's the place where tricksters come to play.

Autumn Tricksters is the second installment in the Year of the Harem collection.

Coming October 2020.

Knights of Winter
A castle in Wales.
A snowstorm.
A legend retold.

Knights of Winter is the third installment of the Year of the Harem collection.

Coming November 2020.

www.ingramcontent.com/pod-product-compliance
Lightning Source LLC
Chambersburg PA
CBHW011433170626
46808CB00010B/3137